A DRAWING FROM LIFE
BY JOHN CECIL CLAY

JAP HERRON

JAP HERRON

A NOVEL WRITTEN FROM
THE OUIJA BOARD

WITH AN INTRODUCTION

THE COMING OF JAP HERRON

APPLEWOOD BOOKS
Carlisle, Massachusetts

THE COMING OF
"JAP HERRON"

On the afternoon of the second Thursday in March,
1915, I responded to an invitation to the regular meeting of a small psychical research society. There was
to be a lecture on cosmic relations, and the hostess
for the afternoon, whom I had met twice socially,
thought I might be interested, my name having appeared in connection with a recently detailed series of
psychic experiments. To all those present, with the
exception of the hostess, I was a total stranger. I
learned, with some surprise, that these men and women
had been meeting, with an occasional break of a few
months, for more than five years. The record of these
meetings filled several type-written volumes.

When word came that the lecturer was unavoidably
detained, the hostess requested Mrs. Lola V. Hays to
entertain the members and guests by a demonstration
of her ability to transmit spirit messages by means of
a planchette and a lettered board. The apparatus was
familiar to me; but the outcome of that afternoon's
experience revealed a new use for the transmission

1

board. After several messages, more or less personal, had been spelled out, the pointer of the planchette traced the words:

"Samuel L. Clemens, lazy Sam." There was a long pause, and then: "Well, why don't some of you say something?"

I was born in Hannibal, and my pulses quickened. I wanted to put a host of questions to the greatest humorist and the greatest philosopher of modern times; but I was an outsider, unacquainted with the usages of the club, and I remained silent while the planchette continued:

"Say, folks, don't knock my memoirs too hard. They were written when Mark Twain was dead to all sense of decency. When brains are soft, the method should be anæsthesia."

Not one of those present had read Mark Twain's memoirs, and the plaint fell upon barren soil. The arrival of the lecturer prevented further confession from the unseen communicant; but I was so deeply impressed that I begged my hostess to permit me to come again. For my benefit a meeting was arranged at which there was no lecturer, and I was asked to sit for the first time with Mrs. Hays.

In my former psychic investigation, it had been my habit to pronounce the letters as the pointer of the planchette indicated them, and Mrs. Hays urged me to render the same service when I sat with her, because she never permitted herself to look at the board, fearing that her own mind would interfere with the transmission.   Scarcely had our finger-tips touched the planchette when it darted to the letters which spelled the words:

"I tried to write a romance once, and the little wife laughed at it.   I still think it is good stuff and I want it written.   The plot is simple.   You'd best skeletonize the plot.   Solly Jenks, Hiram Wall—young men. Time, before the Civil War."

Then the outline of a typical Mark Twain story came in short, explosive sentences.   It was entitled, "Up the Furrow to Fortune."   A brief account of its coming seems vital to the more sustained work which was destined to follow it.   I was not present at the next regular meeting of the society; but at its close I was summoned to the telephone and informed that Mark Twain had come again and had said that "the Hannibal girl" was the one for whom he and Mrs. Hays had been waiting.   When they asked him what he meant, the planchette made reply:

"Consult your record for 1911."

One of the early volumes of the society's record was brought forth, and a curious fact that all the members of the society had forgotten was unearthed.   About a year after his passing out, Mr. Clemens had told Mrs. Hays that he had carried with him much valuable literary material which he yearned to send back, and that he would transmit stories through her, if she could find just the right person to sit with her at the transmission board. Although she experimented with each member of the club, and with several of her friends who were sympathetic though not avowed investigators, he was not satisfied with any of them. Then she gave up the attempt and dismissed it from her mind. A twenty-minute test with me seemed to convince him that in me he had found the negative side of the mysterious human mechanism for which he had been waiting.

The work of transmitting that first story was attended with the greatest difficulty. No less than three distinct styles of diction, accompanied by correspondingly distinct motion in the planchette under our fingers, were thrust into the record. At first we were at a loss to understand these intrusions. That they were intrusions there could be no doubt. In each case there was a sharp deviation from the plot of the story, as it had been given to us in the synopsis. After one of these experiences, which resulted in the introduction of a paragraph that was rather clever but not at all pertinent, Mark regained control with the impatiently traced words:

"Every scribe here wants a pencil on earth."

Not until the middle of summer did we achieve that sureness of touch which now enables us to recognize, intuitively, the presence of the one scribe whose thoughts we are eager to transmit. That the story of Jap Herron and the two short stories which preceded it are the actual post-mortem work of Samuel L. Clemens, known to the world as Mark Twain, we do not for one moment doubt. His individuality has been revealed to us in ways which could leave no question in our minds. The little, intimate touches which reveal personality are really of more importance than the larger and more conspicuous fact that neither Mrs. Hays nor I could have written the fiction that has come across our transmission board. Our literary output is well known, and not even the severest psychological skeptic could assert that it bears any resemblance to the literary style of "Jap Herron."

Mrs. Hays has found the best market for her short stories with one of the large religious publishing houses, and in the early days Mark Twain seemed to fear that her subconscious mind might inadvertently color or distort his thought, in process of transmission. We had come to the end of our fourth session when he added this:

"There will be minor errors that you will be able to take care of. I don't object. Only—don't try to correct my grammar. I know what I want to say. And, dear ladies, when I say d-a-m-n, please don't write d-a-r-n. Don't try to smooth it out. This is not a smooth story."

That Mark should fear the blue pencil, at our hands,

amused us greatly. The story bristles with profanity
and is roughly picturesque in its diction. It deals with
a section of the Ozark country with which neither of
us is familiar, and in the speech of the natives there
are words that we had never heard, that are included
in no dictionary but are, it transpires, perfectly familiar to the primitive people in the southwestern part
of the state. When the revision of the story was almost complete, Mark interrupted the dictation, one
afternoon, to remark:

"You are too tired. Forces must be strong for results. Somebody handed you a lemon, back there. Cut
out that part about the apple at fly time. I am not
carping. You have done well. The interpretation is
excellent. I was afraid of femininity. Women have
their ideas, but this is not a woman's story. Good-
bye."

There was another meeting, at which the revision of
"Up the Furrow to Fortune" was completed, and then
we went to work on the second story, "A Daughter
of Mars." As in the case of the first one, it began with
a partial synopsis. Vallon Leithe, an enthusiastic
aeronaut, was resting after a long flight, when a
strange air-craft fell out of the sky, lodging in the
top of a great tree. The occupant of the marvelously
constructed flying machine proved to be a girl from the
planet Mars. Her name was Ulethe, and she had many

thrilling adventures on our earth.   The synopsis ended with the wholly unexpected words:

"Now, girls, it is not yet clear in my mind whether we'd better send Ulethe back to Mars, kill her, marry her to Leithe, or have an expedition from Mars raise the dickens.   But we will let it develop itself."

The board, on which two short stories and a novel have already been transmitted, is one of the ordinary varieties, a polished surface over which the planchette glides to indicate the letters of the alphabet and the figures from 1 to 10.   In the main our dictation came without any apparent need for marks of punctuation. Occasionally the words "quotation marks," or "Put that in quotes" would be interjected.   Once when my intonation, as I pronounced the words for the amanuensis who was keeping our record, seemed to indicate a direct statement, the planchette whirled under our fingers and traced the crisp statement, "I meant that for a question."

When I told my husband of these grippingly intimate evidences of an unseen personality, it occurred to him that a complete set of punctuation marks, carefully applied in India ink, where the pointer of the planchette could pick them out as they were required, would facilitate the transmission of sustained narrative.   To him it seemed that the absence of these marks on the board must be maddening, especially to Mark Twain, whose thought could be hopelessly distorted by the omission of so trivial a thing as a comma, and whose subtle use of the colon was known to all the clan of printers. Before our next meeting the board had been duly adorned with ten of the most important marks, including the hyphen and the M-dash. The comma was at the head of the right-hand column and the apostrophe at the bottom. My husband, Mrs. Hays and I knew exactly what all these markings meant, yet we had some confusion because Mark insisted on using the comma when he wished to indicate a possessive case. The sentence was this, as I understood it:

"I was not wont to disobey my father, scommand."

Instantly my husband, who had become interested and had taken the place of our first amanuensis, perceived that I had made a mistake, when I pronounced the combination, "f-a-t-h-e-r, comma, s-c-o-m-m-a-n-d."

"But," I defended myself, "the pointer went to the comma. I can see now that it should have been the apostrophe." As I spoke the pointer of the planchette traced the words on the board:

"Edwin did a pretty piece of work, but that apostrophe is too far down. I am in danger of falling off the board every time I make a run for it."

The result was that another apostrophe was placed in the middle of the board, directly under the letter S. In connection with the M-dash we had a yet more startling evidence of an outside personality, one dependent on us for his means of communication, but wholly independent of our thought and knowledge. Mark had dictated the synopsis for the second story and had enlarged upon the first situation. Then, as has since become his fixed habit, he indicated that the serious work for the evening was ended, and returned for an informal chat. Mrs. Hays and I had discussed the plot at some length, and after my husband had read aloud the second evening's dictation we commented on some of the obscure points, our fingers resting, the while, lightly on the planchette. Suddenly it became agitated, assumed a vigorous sweeping motion and traced very rapidly these words:

"It is starting good; but will you two ladies stop speculating? I am going to take care of this story. Don't try to dictate. You are interrupting the thread of the story. There is ample time for smoothing the rough places. I am not caviling. I am well pleased." After a pause, he continued: "There is the same class of interruption—those who could write stories, but are not to write my——" At this, the planchette turned to the M-dash and slid back and forth under it several times. It then spelled the word "stories." We were utterly at a loss, until he explained: "I was using that black line for an underscore."

Again and again we have had the word "good" in an adverbial construction, a usage that is not common to either Mrs. Hays or me; but Mark has told us that he liked it, in familiar conversation. We have tried to adhere with absolute fidelity to even the seeming errors which came over the board.

The second installment of the story gave all of us much trouble. Incidentally it served to develop several bits of humorous conversation. When it was finished, we received this comment:

"I think that is all we can do to-night. I intend to enlarge upon this chapter before going further. The forces are not strong enough to-night. We will re-write this part Monday night."

We naturally expected a rehandling of that installment, which for convenience he had designated a "chapter." To our surprise, the pointer of the planchette gave this:

"I have changed my mind. We will proceed to New York. I will probably want to handle chapter second in a different way. It reads like a printed porous plaster; but that is no one's fault. Begin!"

The dictation went smoothly, and there were no interruptions from the unseen rivals who had so persistently contested Mark Twain's right to the exclusive use of our "pencil." Before the next meeting I was urged to take a prominent part in another piece of psychic work, and to persuade both my husband and Mrs. Hays to join me. I said nothing to either one of them about it, intending to discuss it with them when the evening's work was over. As soon, however, as we applied our finger tips to the planchette, this astonishing communication came:

"I am afraid that my pencil-holders are going to get wound up in other stuff that will make much confusion. I heard Emily talking over the telephone and making promises that are not good for our work."

When I had been questioned concerning the meaning of this rebuke, and had explained its import, Mark added: "If we are going to make good there must be concentration, to that end. Get busy." We did! It was a hot July night, and the planchette flew over the board so swiftly that at times I could scarcely keep pace with it as I pronounced the letters. With other amanuenses I had been forced to pronounce the finished words, and to repeat sentences in whole or in part; but after my husband came into the work this was not necessary. As much as a score of letters might be run together, to be divided into words after the dictation was ended. Sometimes, when I had failed utterly to catch the thought, and would hesitate or ask to have the thing repeated, my husband would say to me: "Don't stop him. I know what it means." Mrs. Hays avoided looking at the board lest her own mind interfere with the transmission, and with less efficient help, the entire responsibility had been on me. When I came to realize that nothing was expected of me beyond the mere pronouncing of the letters, the three of us developed swiftly into a smoothly working

machine. Yet Mark was constantly worried for fear
that my heart would be alienated and that I would "go
chasing after strange gods," as he once put it.

When he had finished the fifth installment of the
story, with a climax that surprised and puzzled us, he
said:

"I reckon we had better lay by for a few days till
I get this thing riffled out. It has slipped its tether.
I have had such things happen often. Don't get
scared."

We discussed the use of the word "riffle," and then
Mark became serious.

"I don't want to be disappointed in the Hannibal
girl. I have been trying for several years to get
through to the light. I don't want a false sentiment
for a crew of fanatics to wreck my chance. I don't
want to act nasty, but if you go into that other work
I am likely to ruin your reputation. You are likely
to explode into some of the mediocre piffle that is the
height and depth of such would-be communications with
the other world. There is nothing to hold to. So, my
dear girls, if you want a future, cut it out. I don't
want to command all your time, but right now it is
best to avoid all complications."

It is needless to say I declined the invitation. After
this, whenever anything went wrong, the rebuke or complaint was invariably addressed to me. When there
were humorous or pleasant things to be said, they were

dispensed equally to the three of us, whom Mark Twain had come to designate as "my office force." Two bits of personal communication came within the succeeding week which seem to have a bearing on the whole mysterious experience. That second installment was undertaken and abandoned again and again. Finally he said:

"I am going ahead with the main body of the story. There will be another round with that second chapter, but not until the theme is fully developed. The second chapter sticks in my throat like the cockleburr that I tried to swallow when I was five. It won't slip down or come up."

We had worked patiently on the latter part of the narrative and had accomplished a big evening's work, when the dictation was interrupted by this remark:

"It is going good; but I sure wish that I had Edwin's pipe."

We fairly gasped with astonishment; but we had no time for comment, as the planchette continued its amazing revelation:

"Smoke up, old man, for auld lang syne. In the other world they don't know Walter Raleigh's weed, and I have not found Walter yet to make complaint. I forget about it till I get Edwin's smoke. But for pity's sake, Ed, cut out that tobacco you were trying out. It made me sick. I hoped it would get you, so that you wouldn't try it again."

My husband, whom neither Mrs. Hays nor I would, under any circumstances, address by the abbreviation of his name, "Ed," asked Mark what tobacco he had in mind. He replied:

"That packet you were substituting, or that some one that had a grudge against you gave you."

A comparison of dates revealed the fact that on the evening when that troublesome second installment was transmitted, my husband had smoked some heavy imported tobacco that had been given to him by a friend he had met that afternoon. The circumstance had passed from the minds of all of us. Indeed, it had never impressed us in the least, and it had not occurred to any of us that our unseen visitor still retained the sense of smell, or that he could distinguish between two brands of tobacco. He had given evidence of both sight and hearing, had told us frequently that he was tired, at the end of a long evening's work, and had made other incidental revelations of his environment and condition: but his reference to the pipe was more significant than any of them.

Early in August, when our second story was nearing completion, the transmission began with this curious bit, which none of us understood for a long time:

"Emily, I think that when we finish this story we will do a pastoral of Missouri. There appear high lights and shadows, purple and dark, and the misty pink of dawnings that make world-weary ones have surcease."

Not until "Jap Herron" was more than half finished did we realize that it was the Missouri pastoral. There was one other veiled reference to that story which must not be omitted. We had planned a trip to New York, for some time in October or early November, although we had never discussed it while at the board. One evening Mark terminated his dictation abruptly, and said:

"Emily, I think well of your plan." I asked what plan he referred to. "New York. I will go, too. I will try to convince them that I am not done working. I am rejuvenated and want to finish my work. When I was in New York last I had a very beautiful dream. I did not understand it then. It meant that my days were numbered, and gave me the picture of an angel bringing a book from heaven to earth, and on its cover was blazoned this: MARK TWAIN'S COMPLIMENTS. Ask them what they think about that. I was so tired—so tired that I could not rest. A cool hand seemed to soothe my weariness away and I slept, and, sleeping, dreamed."

When I found that passage in the early part of our record, I wondered if "Jap Herron" might be the book sent to earth with Mark Twain's compliments. I asked him about it, one evening when our regular dictation had been finished. The reply was a slow journey of the planchette to the word, "Yes," followed by the rapidly spelled words, "But old Mark isn't done talking yet."

We assumed that he had something further to say to us, and when I asked him what he wanted to talk about, he gave this tantalizing reply:

"Curious? Wait and see." Then, after a pause, "I shall have other work for my office force."

The explanation of this cryptic statement was not given until we had completed the final revision of the story. Before I reveal what he had in mind, I wish to state that which is to me the most convincing proof of the supernormal origin of the three stories that had been traced, letter by letter, on our transmission board. That they come through Mrs. Hays, there can be no doubt whatever. My total lack of psychic power has been abundantly demonstrated. Mrs. Hays has written much light fiction; but it is necessary for her to write a story at one sitting. If it does not come "all in one piece" it is foredoomed to failure. I know nothing of Mark Twain's habits; but in all the work we have done for him, the first draft has been rough and vigorous, and sweeping changes have been made by him while the work was undergoing revision. In the case of "Jap Herron" some of the most important changes were made without a rereading of the story, changes that involved incidents which we had forgotten, and for which I was compelled to search the original record. When I had substituted these passages for the ones they were to supplant, I made a typewritten copy of the entire story and we read it aloud to Mark. Mrs. Hays

and I sat with our finger tips on the planchette so
that he could interrupt; but he made only a few minor
corrections.   The story had been virtually rewritten
twice, although a few of the chapters, as they now
stand, are exactly as they were transmitted, not so
much as a word having been changed.   The only change
made in the fourteenth chapter came near the end,
where Mark had suggested a line of dashes or stars to
bridge the break between Jap's leaving his mother and
the announcement that his mother was dead.   Forty-
eight words were dictated to show what Jap actually
did, in that painful interim, the three sentences being
rounded out by the words, "There, I think that sounds
better."

Sometimes, in the course of the revision, we have
been interrupted by the jerkily traced words, "Try
this," or "We'll fix that better," or "I told Emily to
take out those repetitions."   It has happened that he
used the same word four times in one paragraph, and
in copying I have substituted the obvious synonym.
Occasionally he did not approve of my correction and
would rebuke me sharply.   In the main he has expressed
himself as well pleased with the labor I have spared
him.   On the 10th of January, 1916, Mrs. Hays came
to my home for a last reading of the finished manu-
script.   When she read it through, I asked her to sit
at the board with me.   There was something about
which I wanted to question Mark, and I did not wish

her mind to interfere in any way with the answer. Mrs.
Hays had had two curious psychic experiences in connection with our work. The first came to her when we
were still at work on "A Daughter of Mars." It was
in the form of a vivid dream in which Mark Twain said
to her, "Don't be discouraged, Lola. All that we have
done in the past is just forging the hammer for the
larger strokes we are going to make." The second
was similar; but the man who appeared to her was a
stocky, bald-headed man in a frock coat. When she
asked him who he was and what he wanted, he replied,
"Mark Twain sent me to call on you."

At this time, "Jap Herron" was being revised, and
she supposed that this man, with the striking personality, would be introduced somewhere. However, the
story was ended, and no such character had appeared.
I wanted to know whether or not the dream was significant. I said:

"Mark, did you ever send anybody to call on Lola?"
The planchette replied:

"Yes, I sent him. We will do another story. We
will wait until the smoke of this one clears away. I
want Emily to have a rest, and many other things will
be adjusted. I would like to have my old office force.
It is to be a bigger book than this one—more important. The man I sent you was Brent Roberts."

We dropped our hands in amazement. Brent Roberts appears twice in the Jap Herron story. He is not

half so conspicuous as Holmes, the saloon-keeper, or
Hollins, the grocer.   In truth, we had scarcely noticed
him.   I asked:

"Mark, are you going to give a sequel to 'Jap Herron'?"   He said:

"No.   Brent Roberts had a story before he elected
to spend his last years in Bloomtown.   Now, girls, don't
speculate.   I am taking care of Brent Roberts."

He added that it was "up to Emily" to give his book
to the world, and that he intended to explore a little
of the Uncharted Country while he was waiting for
his office force to resume work.   Once I asked him, while
he was transmitting "A Daughter of Mars," whether
he had ever visited that planet.   He replied:

"No, this is pure fiction.   I elected to return to
earth.   I wanted to take the taste of those memoirs out
of my mouth."

One other passage from the early record may profit-
ably precede the actual story of Jap's coming.   We
were in the midst of the most critical revision.   My
husband was commanded to read the story, paragraph
by paragraph.   When there was no comment, the planchette remained motionless under our fingers, but there
were few passages that escaped some change.   Several
times the changed wording conflicted with something
farther along in the story, and it was necessary to go
back and make another correction.   The revision sheets
covered a big table, and my husband found it very

exasperating to make the corrections. At length Mark said:

"Smoke up and cool off, old boy. Perhaps I should apologize. The last secretary I had used to wear an ice-soaked towel inside his head. The girls and old Mark together make a riffle. Well, we will slow up. In my ambition, I have been too eager. It is hard to explain how great a thing is the power to project my mentality through the clods of oblivion. I have so long sought for an opening. Be patient, please. I am not carping. I get Edwin's position. We will be easy with the new saddle, so the nag won't run away. I heard Edwin's suggestion, and it is a good one. We will go straight through the story, beginning where we left off to-night. That was what I intended to do, but that second chapter nipped me."

When next we met we had no thought of any other work than the revision of the story on which we had been working at frequent intervals for about two months. We never knew whether a session at the board would begin with a bit of personal conversation or a prolonged stretch of dictation. We held ourselves passive, ready to fall in with the humor or whim of our astonishingly human though still intangible guest. The beginning of that evening's work—it was the 6th of September—was almost too great an upheaval for me. The planchette fairly raced as it spelled the words:

"This story will have legitimate chapters. Nosy nopsis. Then ameisjapherron. Begin. Asevery well-bred story has a hero, and as the reseems better material in jap than in any other party to this story, we will dignify him."

I wanted to stop, but my husband insisted that I make no break in the impatient dictation. He had perceived that the first string of letters spelled the words, "No synopsis. The name is Jap Herron," but I could not see his copy, and to my mind the sentences spelled chaos. A little farther along I ventured an interruption, when we had transmitted the sentence, "The folks in Happy Hollow continued to say Magnesia long after she left its fragrant depths." I had just spelled out the name, Agnesia, and I was too deeply engrossed with the labor of following the letters to even attempt to understand the meaning. I turned to my husband and said:

"It probably didn't intend to stop on that letter M," whereat the planchette rebuked my stupidity thus: "Emily, they called her Magnesia."

After that, I contrived to get control of my nerves, and the rest of the dictation was not so difficult. When we had received the crisp final sentence, "And stay he did," the planchette went right on with this information, "This is the first copy of the first chapter. There will be 25 or more chapters. This is enough for this time, as the office force is a little weak. But results

. . . very good. We will finish the other story and dip into this at the next session. There will be better speed in this, for there will be no revision until it is finished. We will work hard and fast. Emily may meet folks she knows in this tale, for she knows a town with a river and a Happy Hollow. I did not intend to start another story so soon, but other influences are so strong that they may try to dominate the board. This will not tire you so much. You must be determined not to permit intruders. If they are recognized, you will not be free of them again. I am pushed aside. Leave the board when they appear. Good-bye."

The use of the name, Happy Hollow, forms a link with Hannibal; but if any of the characters in "Jap Herron" were drawn from life, they must have belonged to Mark Twain's generation and not to mine. Mark never seems to take into account the fact that he left Hannibal before I was born, and that there have been many changes in the old town. The character of Jacky Herron may have been suggested by a disreputable drunken fisherman whose experiences I have heard my father relate; but there is one little touch in that first chapter that must have come from Mark's own mind, since the underlying fact was not known to any of us until we read Walter Prichard Eaton's article on birds' nests, months later. When we transmitted that statement, "The father of the little Herrons was a king-fisher," none of us knew that the kingfisher's home nest is a filthy hole, close to the river bank. The application is too perfect to have been accidental.

Before another chapter of the story was transmitted, I went to spend a morning with Mrs. Hays. At the request of her son, we consented to allay his curiosity by a visible demonstration of the workings of the mysterious board, of which he had necessarily heard much. He hoped to receive some definite communication from his father, or the sister who had died in her girlhood; but this is what he recorded:

"Emily, I gave those synopses not for a guide but to prevent others from imposing their ideas and confusing you. It might be said that it made it easier for you, but that idea is wrong. It would be easier to write the story direct. You have learned that this was wise, because constant efforts have been made to break in and alter the stories. For this reason I gave you the synopses, so that you could not be deceived. Now I am going to trust you. I intended to advise you that it would be a more convincing psychic record, if you have nothing on which a subconscious mind might be said to be working. The synopsis was for your protection, and has no value to the record. At first you had such a conglomerate method of working that it was necessary. You did not recognize the difficulties that were likely to occur. You were apt to employ temporary help, so eliminate."

Just what was meant by "temporary help" is not

apparent; but there was no opportunity to question him further, for at that moment we were interrupted by the arrival of another luncheon guest and the board was put aside. We devoted two sessions to the revision and finishing touches of the troublesome short story, and then we plunged into the transmission of "Jap Herron" in deadly earnest.

As far as possible, we sat twice a week, on Mondays and Fridays. We usually worked uninterruptedly for two hours, with no sound save that of my voice as I pronounced the letters and punctuation marks over which the pointer of the planchette paused in its swift race across the board. My husband discovered early in the work that if he permitted himself the luxury of a smile he was in danger of distracting Mrs. Hays, who always sat facing him, and thus of bringing about confusion in the record. Under Mark's specific instruction she has schooled herself to keep her mind as nearly blank as is possible for a woman who is absolutely conscious and normal, and the evidence that something humorous was being transmitted through her would be diverting, to say the least. As for my own part in the work, I seldom realized the import of the sentences I had spelled out, my whole attention being concentrated on the rapidly gliding pointer. When my husband read aloud the copy he had taken down it almost invariably came to Mrs. Hays and me as something entirely new.

The story of Jap Herron, as it stands completed, does not follow the original order of the first fifteen chapters. The early part of the tale was handled in a manner so sketchy and rapid in its action that three whole chapters and seven fragments of chapters were dictated and inserted after the work was finished. In the original copy the second chapter suffered little change up to the point of George Thomas's advent, with the suggestion that he might bring in some more turnips. Following the disaster to Judge Bowers's speech, Mark took a short cut to pave the way for the next chapter. It ran thus:

"But bad luck cannot camp on your trail forever. In the gladsome June-time, Ellis married Flossy Bowers, and her dowry of two thousand dollars and her following of kin set the *Herald* on its feet."

These two sentences were expanded into the more important half of the third chapter, almost five months after they had been dictated, and this without a rereading of the story. At another time, when this curious kind of revision was under way, Mark dictated the latter part of the second chapter, wherein Ellis Hinton tells Jap how he happened to be starving in Bloomtown. When he had finished the dictation, with the words, "My boy, that blue calico lady was Mrs. Kelly Jones," he continued:

"Emily will know where to fit it in."

This fitting in was not extremely difficult, since there

was only one place in the story into which each of the
inserted chapters or fragments could be made to fit;
but the original copy had to be read several times
before these thin places became apparent, and I got
no help whatever from Mark. Once, when I implored
him to tell me where a certain brief but gripping paragraph belonged, he replied, "Emily, that is your
job. I don't want the Hannibal girl to fall down on it."

On that second Monday night in September, when
the "office force" settled itself to serious work, my
husband read to us the copy we had transmitted. The
chapter ended with what is now the closing paragraph
of the third chapter:

"The *Herald* put on a new dress, and the hell-box was
dumped full of the discarded, mutilated types that had
so long given strabismus to the patient readers of the
Bloomtown *Herald*."

The diet of turnips and sorghum and the other
humorous touches of the narrative overwhelmed us with
laughter, whereat the planchette under our fingers
wrote:

"Sounds like Mark, eh?"

I asked him if he was satisfied with the use of the word
"Herald" twice in that last sentence. He replied:
"You must excuse me. I am all in. I told you I would
leave minor points to your pencil. T-i-r-e-d. Good-
bye."

Our first acquaintance with Wat Harlow, as he appeared in the fourth chapter, gave little promise of the character into which he was destined to be developed. To the three of us, who laughed over the episode of the vermilion handbill, he appeared to be nothing more than a third-rate country politician. In the original transcription he received only an occasional passing touch, until the death of Ellis brought him forth in a new light. We did not know then what Ellis had meant by "that reformed auctioneer," for the story of Wat's connection with the upbuilding of Bloomtown, as it is set forth in the sixth chapter, was not told until we were well along with the work of revision.

One of the most interesting personal touches, to be found only in our private record, was introduced at the end of the fourth chapter. It had been a long stretch of dictation, and when the planchette stopped I asked if there was any more. The pointer gave only this, "No—30." Having had no experience with printing offices, I was mystified until my husband explained that "30 on the hook" means the end of a given piece of work.

Mark once made use of the expression, "the story contains a great deal of brevity that will have to be untied later on." This untying process is nowhere more aptly illustrated than in the fourth chapter of our original copy, a brief chapter that contained the condensed material of Wat Harlow's letter to Jap, the birth of little J.W. and Isabel Granger's first kiss.

There was nothing about Bill's boyhood, no record of Jap's home surroundings, none of the amusing details of the printing office wherein Jap and Bill were learning their trade. All these incidents, which seem so essential to the story, were introduced when the first draft of the story had been completed. The seventh chapter, which has to do with the babyhood of little J.W., was dictated after the revision had apparently been completed. When I asked Mark why he inserted it, the planchette made this curious reply:

"I was thinking that we'd better soften the shock of the boy's death."

For us, through whom the story was being transmitted, there was no softening of Ellis Hinton's death. We knew from the foregoing chapter that the country editor had gone to the mountains for his health, and that Flossy had no hope; but when we had recorded the words: "Jap closed the press upon the inky type, and gathered the great bunches of fragrant blossoms and heaped them upon the press, to be forever silent," a great wave of sadness swept over me, I knew not why. The action of the planchette was so rapid that I could not stop to think or question. It was as if the man dictating the story had an unpleasant task before him, which he wished to have done with as soon as possible. When the final words, "At rest. Flossy," had been spelled out, and the planchette stopped abruptly, Mrs. Hays cried:

"My God, what has happened!" and I looked up to see that she was very white, and tears were slipping down her cheeks.

"Ellis is dead," my husband said, very simply. He had foreseen the end, had grasped the infinite pathos of that old Washington press, decked as a funeral casket with the flowers that had been sent to usher in the new régime.

When the evening's copy had been read, I asked Mark if he wished to comment on it.

"Not to-night, Emily," the planchette spelled. "I am all broken up. I didn't want Ellis to die. I tried to figure a way to save him; but I couldn't make it go."

When we met again, on the 2d of October, the dictation began with these words:

"I want Edwin to go back to the beginning of the last chapter. I left out a sentence that is necessary. It explains why Ellis left by rail. You insert."

Then he dictated the passage relating to the new railroad and the temporary station. When he had finished he said, "Go on with the story," and the next sentence began, "When Ellis went away it was to the sound of jollity." The reference to Robert Louis Stevenson was new to both of us, and we have not sought to verify the incident. That Mark wanted it included in his story was sufficient for us.

That next chapter contained another accumulation of brevity which was afterward untied. The funeral, the reading of Ellis Hinton's will, Judge Bowers's candidacy, the nomination of Jap Herron as the ugliest man in Bloomtown, Bill's first spree and the local option fight, all these were sketched with the sharpness and sudden transition of pictures on a cinematograph screen. The following chapter was almost as tightly packed with incident, and in the midst of it there was a break, with an astonishing explanation. Three evenings in succession we had had trouble with the planchette. It had seemed to me that Mrs. Hays was trying to pull it from beneath my fingers. Meanwhile she had mentally accused me of digital heaviness. She uses the finger tips of her left hand while I use my right. As a rule our touch is so light that the planchette glides automatically. On these three evenings we had left the board with cramped fingers, and a general sense of dissatisfaction. Several sentences that were plainly spurious were afterward stricken from the record; but we had forgotten about the other scribes who wanted "a pencil on earth," until Mark interrupted the story to say:

"I must ask you to be wary and sharp to dismiss impostors. Right now there are more than twenty hands trying to control your dictation. It is very hard for me. I am disconsolate, and powerless to help myself. If we do not watch every avenue, our work is spoiled. There has been a constant struggle for my rights. I only ask a little help, and you are all my hope. If you fail me, I am undone."

This illuminating outburst served to clear the atmosphere, and the three chapters were afterward expanded into seven, much of the same diction being reproduced. It was as if Mark, knowing the difficulties on his own side of the shadow-line, had tried to get at least the outline of his story down on paper, lest he lose his hold entirely. After that evening we had almost no trouble with intruders.

The story of Jones, of the Barton *Standard,* came to us like a thunder clap from a cloudless sky, for the part which old Pee-Dee Jones played in the development of Bloomtown and Barton was not related until we had begun the work of revision. In the original story of that near-fight, Mark gave us a significant cross-light on the conditions under which he lives. The marshal had appeared in the office at the crucial moment, as if he had dropped through the roof or arisen out of the floor. Several times in the earlier part of the work the characters had thus appeared without obvious means of locomotion, and I had called attention to the inconsistency, with the result that Mark had dictated a few words to show how or whence the new arrival had come. When Wilfred Jones shouted to the marshal, "I demand protection," my husband, who was reading the evening's copy aloud to us, said:

"How does the marshal happen to be there? I don't see any previous mention of him."

Instantly the planchette, which we always kept in readiness under our finger tips, began to move. It dictated this:

"You might say, 'at that moment the town marshal, wearing his star pinned to his blue flannel shirt, strolled in.' I have been away from the need of going up-stairs and down-stairs for so long that I forget about it."

"How do you get from one place to another, Mark?" I asked.

"Now, Emily, curiosity! But you know we haven't any Pullman cars or elevators here. When I want to be at a place where I am free to go—why, I am there."

He took occasion, when our difficulties seemed to be at an end and his grip on his "pencil" was once more firmly established, to make it very plain to me that I alone was responsible for the annoyance we had had. He put it thus:

"Things will be all right if you don't give way to any more curiosity. In the beginning I told you that it would not do. Emily wants to investigate too much. It must be one or all. Edwin and I understand. It was you that mixed the type. Lola must be passive. If she tries to watch for intruders, she gets in my way. So it is up to the Hannibal girl."

I do not know, even now, how I could have prevented

the trouble that well-nigh wrecked our work. It is true I had taken part in another psychic demonstration, but it was in a remote part of the city and it had nothing to do with Mark Twain's "pencil." However, I took no further chance with psychic investigation.

When Jap Herron was elected Mayor of Bloomtown, and the girl he loved had walked right into his astonished arms, it seemed to us that the story must be ended. We had forgotten that Jap ever had a family of his own, a mother and two sisters, and when the drunken hag reeled into the *Herald* office we were as greatly horrified as Jap himself was. I had put my husband's carefully kept copy into type-written form, and it occurred to me to get the opinion of a master critic on the story, not as evidence of the survival of the human mind after physical death, but as pure fiction. Acting upon the impulse, and without telling either my husband or Mrs. Hays what I intended to do, I took the copy to William Marion Reedy,[1] permitting him to infer that I had created it, and asked him to tell me whether, in his judgment, the story was worth

[1] William Marion Reedy, Editor and Publisher of *Reedy's Mirror*, a weekly journal published in St. Louis, has long been interested in psychic phenomena, as a source of exotic and unusual literature. He has also discovered and developed much purely terrestrial literary talent, having brought out some of the best poets and fiction writers of present-day America. As a critic, he is a recognized master.

finishing. It was the beginning of the week, when the issuing of the *Mirror* consumed all his time, and while I was waiting for his verdict we received three more chapters. In the first of these we had a new light on Isabel Granger's character, and came for the first time absolutely to love Bill Bowers. After that nothing that Bill might do would shake our faith in his ability to make good in the end. He might be weak and foolish, but we understood why Jap believed in and loved him. We were jubilant when Rosy Raymond was eliminated from the game, for we feared, whenever we permitted ourselves to speculate, that Bill would marry her, and regret the step. We assumed that the son of the much-married Judge Bowers had inherited a nature sufficiently mobile to recover from the shock of the silly girl's perfidy.

While this unexpected development of the story was being revealed to us, William Marion Reedy sent me, in the envelope with the first ten chapters of "Jap Herron," a criticism that fairly made me tingle with delight. Had the work been my own, I could not have been more pleased with his unstinted praise. I wanted to go to him at once and confess the truth; but he was not in his office when I called.

Two of the succeeding chapters were taken down by friends who had been let into the secret of our work and had asked permission to sit with us. It was the time of year when my husband could seldom spare an evening from his work, and Mark consented to break into his beloved office-force arrangement, for the sake of expediency. Three men and five women served us in the capacity of amanuenses while the latter third of the book was being transmitted. The first deviation from our original arrangement came in connection with the dictation of the seventeenth chapter, the chapter that ends with the death of Flossy and her son. We were three sympathetic women, and when the planchette had traced the words, "It was a smile of heavenly beauty, as the pure soul of Ellis Hinton's wife flew to join her loved ones," we three burst simultaneously into violent weeping. I have never experienced more genuine grief at the grave of a departed friend or relative than I felt when this woman, who had come to be more than human to me, was released from her envelope of mortal clay.

The following day Mrs. Hays and I were invited to the home of a delightful little Scotch woman who asked us to bring the planchette board. She knew nothing of the story, and had no intimation of the personality on the other side who was sending it across, through our planchette; nevertheless she was willing to keep copy for us. The chapter she wrote down is the eighteenth in the finished story, Jap's funeral sermon and Isabel's song beside Flossy's coffin. Even now I cannot think of that scene without a swelling of the

throat and a blinding rush of tears. It is needless
to say we wept when the dictation was ended.

When our hostess had read aloud the copy I asked
our invisible companion if he had anything more to say.
I avoided mentioning his name, for we did not wish his
identity disclosed. The planchette traced the curious
words:

"You know that the air gets pretty damp for an
old boy after this."

I looked out of the window. It was a murky November afternoon, and I asked, "Do you feel the dampness
of the material atmosphere?" Like a flash came the
reply:

"Emily, girl, you have been getting sob stuff."

Then I yearned to get my fingers in his shock of
white hair, for I knew Mark Twain was laughing at me.
But I had that which gave me consolation, for I had
brought with me Mr. Reedy's letter, analyzing and
commenting upon the story that Mark had created.
Incidentally Mrs. Reedy had asked Mrs. Hays and me
to come to her home the following day to luncheon. I
had told her that Mrs. Hays possessed a high degree
of psychic power, and I consented to bring our board
for a demonstration. I wanted to see Mr. Reedy alone
and explain to him that "Jap Herron" had come to
us over that insensate board, but opportunity was
denied me. As soon as luncheon was over we went
up to that beautiful yellow room in which the best of

Reedy's Mirror is created, and Mrs. Hays and I placed the board on our knees. As soon as Mr. Reedy's fountain pen was ready for action our planchette began:

"Well, I should doff my plaidie and don a kirtle, for 'tis not the sands o' Dee but the wearing o' the green." There was a wide sweep of the planchette, and then, " 'Tis not the shine of steel that always reflects; but it is the claymore that cuts. Both are made of steel and both will mirror sometimes the shillalah. Yet the shillalah is better than the claymore, for the man that is cut will run; but if ye slug him with the blackthorn he will have to listen. This is just a flicker of high light. Bill jumped from bed as the rattle of the latch announced the arrival of a visitor."

My heart thumped wildly for a moment, then sank. I knew that the Bill referred to was Bill Bowers, and not the editor whom hundreds delight to call "Bill Reedy," and I knew, too, that it would be only a moment until he must realize that the sentences he was writing down from my dictation were part and parcel of the story whose first ten chapters he had read and praised. I dared not lift my eyes from the board, yet I wanted to stop and explain that I had not intended to deceive him—that I only wanted an unbiased opinion of Mark Twain's story. In vain I tried to stop the whirling planchette, my voice so husky that I could scarcely pronounce the letters. It went right on, with

a situation that neither Mrs. Hays nor I had anticipated. We had schooled ourselves not to speculate,
yet the previous afternoon we had left Jap in a fainting
condition and on the verge of a long illness. The chapter we transmitted that day was the story of a gubernatorial election in a small Missouri town.

Subsequently, when Mark gave us the intervening
chapter, Jap's visit to the cemetery and the humorous
incidents of the campaign, I asked him:

"Why didn't you give this chapter last Thursday?"

"I thought that election would amuse Reedy. Don't
worry, Emily. He understood you. He knows the
Hannibal girl is honest," was the comforting reply.

When the revision of the story was under way, and
several fragments had been dictated, the planchette
spelled the words, "I want to add something to the
Reedy chapter," and without further ado it proceeded:
"The Bloomtown *Herald* did itself proud that week."
That fragment was the easiest of them all to fit into
place. At its conclusion we were favored with a bit
of pleasantry that seems significant. My husband gave
us a lift whenever he could spare the time; but on this
occasion a woman friend was sitting with us. She had
written about two thousand words of copy, when the
tenor of the dictation changed suddenly to the personal vein.

"Old Mark has been working like a badger, and is
pleased with the story. The girls and friend Ed are

going as well as Twain ever did when he wielded his own pen. When Edwin lights up a fresh smoke and smiles, I know that all is well. But when Lola frowns and Edwin forgets to smoke, look out for leaks. The story has sprung and therain was hesitthininspots." The last of the sentence came so rapidly that none of us had any idea what it meant, or that it meant anything at all. Before we had separated it into the words, "the rain washes it thin in spots," I asked that that last part be repeated. Instead we got the words:

"When a board is sprung, it lets in rain. It is Emily who has to hold the drip pan for the temperamental ones."

"Thank you for those few kind words, Mark," I said. "But if you think enough of me to trust me with this important work, why do you single me out for all the scoldings, when Edwin and Lola sometimes deserve at least a share in your displeasure?"

"Whist, Hannibal girl, we know our office force," was the humorous rejoinder.

The appearance of Agnesia was one of the keen surprises of the story, and before we realized what Jap's little sister would mean to Bloomtown, Mark interrupted his dictation with the words, "Stop! Girls, the yarn is nearly all unwound. We will skip a bit that we will tie in later. But now—Bill sat doubled over the case, the stick held listlessly in his hand. Nervously he fingered the copy, not knowing what he was reading."

Without a break, we received the brief final chapter, ending with the words, "Isabel wants to call him Jasper William." The planchette added, "The End." We transmitted no more that day, although we knew that our story was far from completion.

The next time we met we had another surprise in the coming of Jap's elder sister. When the twenty-fifth chapter was finished, Mark said:

"Girls, I think the story is done."

"It's pretty short for a book," I protested. By way of reply, he gave this:

"Did you ever know about my prize joke? One day I went to church, heard a missionary sermon, was carried away—to the extent of a hundred dollars. The preacher kept talking. I reduced my ante to fifty dollars. He talked on. I came down to twenty-five, to ten, to five, and after he had said all that he had in him, I stole a nickel from the basket. Reason for yourselves. Not how long but how strong. Yet I have a sneaking wish to tell you something of the early days of Ellis's work, especially about Granger and Blanke. But to-day I have writer's cramp. So let's get together soon and make the finish complete."

There were two more sessions, with the dictation of a whole chapter and several fragments, at each meeting, and we met no more until I had put the whole complex record into consecutive form. We had a final review of the work, and a few minor changes in words and phrases were made. Mark expressed himself as well pleased, and as a little farewell he gave us this, which has nothing to do with Jap Herron:

"There will be a great understanding some day. It will come when the earth realizes that we must leave it, to live, and when it can put itself in touch with the heavens that surround it. I have met a number of preachers over here who would like to undo many things they promulgated while they had a whack at sinners.

"There are hardshell Baptists who have a happy time meeting their members, to whom they preached hell and brimstone. They have many things to explain. There is one melancholy Presbyterian who frankly stated the fact—underscore 'fact'—that there were infants in hell not an ell long. He has cleared out quite a space in hell since he woke up. He doesn't rush out to meet his congregation. It would create trouble and be embarrassing if they looked around for the suffering infants. As I said before, there is everything to learn, after the shackles of earth are thrown aside. I would like to write a story about some of these preachers, and the mistakes they made, when the doctrines of brimstone and everlasting punishment were ladled out as freely to the little maid who danced as to the harlot. It showed a mind asleep to the undiscovered country."

"Can you shed any light on that undiscovered country?" I asked him.

"Perhaps. But for the present there is enough of the truth of life and death in 'Jap Herron' to hold you."

And with that he told us good-bye.

EMILY GRANT HUTCHINGS.

JAP HERRON

CHAPTER I

As every well-bred story has a hero, and as there seems better material in Jap than any other party to this story, we will dignify him. Mary Herron feebly asserted her rights in the children by naming them respectively, Fanny Maud, Jasper James and Agnesia. Jasper deteriorated. He became Jap, and Jap he remained, despite the fact that Fanny Maud developed into Fannye Maude and Agnesia changed her cognomen, without recourse to law, to Mabelle. The folks in Happy Hollow continued to say "Magnesia" long after she left its fragrant depths.

The father of the little Herrons was a kingfisher. He spent his hours of toil on the river bank and his hours of ease in Mike's place. One Friday, good luck peered through the dingy windows of the little shanty where the Herrons starved, froze or sweltered. It was Friday, as I remarked before. Mary was washing, against difficulties. It had rained for a week. The clothes had to dry before Mary could cash her labor,

and it fretted Jacky Herron sorely. His credit had
lost caste with Mike, and Mike had the grip on the
town. He had the only thirst parlor in Happy Hollow. So Jacky smashed the only remaining window,
broke the family cup, and set forth defiantly in the
rain. And in the fog and slashing rain he lost his
footing, and fell into the river. As it was Friday, Mary
had hopefully declared that luck would change—and it
did!

The town buried Jacky and moved his family into
decent lodgings, because the Town Fathers did not
want to contract typhoid in ministering to them.
Loosed of the incubus of a father, the little family
grew in grace. Jappie, as his baby sister called him,
was the problem. Agnesia was pretty, and the Mayor's
wife adopted her. Fanny Maud went west to live with
her aunt, and Jap remained with his mother until she,
after the manner of womankind, who never know when
they have had luck, married another bum and began
supporting him. Jap ran away.

He was twelve years old, red-headed, freckled and
lanky, when he trailed into Bloomtown. He loafed
along the main street until he reached the printing
office, and there he stopped. An aphorism of his late
lamented dad occurred to him.

"Ef I had a grain of gumption," said dad, during
an enforced session of his family's society, "I would
'a' went to work in my daddy's printin' office, instid of

runnin' away when I was ten year old. I might 'a' had money, aplenty, 'stid of bein' cumbered and helt down by you and these brats."

Jap straggled irregularly inside and heard the old Washington hand press groan and grunt its weary way through the weekly edition of the *Herald*. After the last damp sheet had been detached from the press, and the papers were being folded by the weary-eyed, inky demon who had manipulated the handle, he slouched forward.

"Say, Mister," he asked confidently, "do you do that every day?" indicating the press, " 'cause I'm goin' to work for you."

The editor, pressman and janitor looked upon him in surprise and pity.

"I appreciate your ambition," he said, more in sorrow than anger, "but I have become so attuned to starving alone that I don't think I could adjust myself to the shock of breaking my fast on you."

Jap was unmoved.

"My dad onct thought he'd be a editor, but he got married," he said calmly.

"Sensible dad," commented the editor, with more truth than he dreamed. "I suppose that he had three meals a day, and a change of socks on Sunday."

"But Ma had to get 'em," argued Jap. "I want to be a editor, and I am agoin' to stay." And stay he did.

CHAPTER II

"Run out and get a box of sardines," ordered the boss of the Washington press. "I've got a nickel. I can't let you starve. I lived three months on them— look at me!"

Jap surveyed him apprehensively.

"I'd hate to be so thin," he complained, "and I don't like sardines nor any fishes. My dad fed us them every day. Allus wanted to taste doughnuts. Can I buy them?"

Ellis Hinton laughed shortly, and spun the nickel across the imposing stone. Jap caught it deftly. An hour later he appeared for work, smiling cheerfully.

"Why the shiner?" queried Ellis, indicating a badly swollen and rapidly discoloring eye.

"Kid called me red-top," said Jap bluntly.

"Love o' gracious," Ellis exclaimed, "what *is* the shade?"

"It's red," quoth Jap, "but it ain't his business. If I am agoin' to be a editor, nobody's goin' to get familiar with me."

This was Jap's philosophy, and in less than a week he had mixed with every youth of fighting age in town.

The office took on metropolitan airs because of the rush of indignant parents who thronged its portals. Ellis pacified some of the mothers, outtalked part of the fathers and thrashed the remainder. After he had mussed the outer office with "Judge" Bowers, and tipped the case over with the final effort that threw him, Jap said, solemnly surveying the wreck:

"If I had a dad like you, I'd 'a' been the President some day."

Ellis gazed ruefully into the mess of pi, and kicked absently at the hell-box.

"I'll work all night," cried Jap eagerly. "I'll clean it up."

"We'll have plenty of time," said Ellis gloomily. "We have to hit the road, kid. Judge Bowers owns the place. He has promised to set us out before morning."

But luck came with Jap. It was Friday again, and Bowers's wife presented him with twins, his mother-in-law arrived, and his uncle inherited a farm. There was only one way for the news to be disseminated, and he came in with his truculent son and helped clean up, so that the *Herald* could be issued on time. More than that, he made the boys shake hands, and concluded to put Bill to work in the *Herald* office. After he had puffed noisily out, Ellis looked whimsically at Bill.

"Are you going to board yourself out of what I am able to pay you?" he asked.

"Oh, I don't reckon Pappy cares about that," the boy said cheerfully. "He just wants to keep me out of mischief, and he said that lookin' at you was enough to sober a sot."

Months dragged by. Bill and Jap worked more or less harmoniously. Once a day they fought; but it was fast becoming a mere function, kept up just for form. Ellis was doing better. He had set up housekeeping, since Jap came, in the back room of the little wooden structure that faced the Public Square, and housewives sent them real food once in a while.

Once Ellis feared that Jap was going to quit him for the Golden Shore. It was on the occasion of Myrtilla Botts's wedding, when she baked the cakes herself, for practice, and her mother thoughtfully sent most of them to the Editor, to insure a big puff for Myrtilla. Ellis was afraid; but Jap, with the enthusiasm and inexperience of youth, took a chance. Bill was laid up with mumps, or the danger would have been lessened. As it was, it took all the doctors in town to keep Jap alive until they could uncurl him and straighten out his appendix, which appeared to be cased in wedding cake. This experience gave Jap an added distaste for the state of matrimony.

"My dad allus said to keep away from marryin',"

he moaned. "But how'd I know you'd ketch it from the eatin's?"

The subscription list grew apace. There was a load of section ties, two bushel of turnips and six pumpkins paid in November. Bill and Jap went hunting once a week, so the larder grew beyond sardines. Jap acquired a hatred of turnips and pumpkins that was in after years almost a mania. At Christmas, Kelly Jones brought in a barrel of sorghum, "to sweeten 'em," he guffawed. Jap had grown to manhood before he wholly forgave that pleasantry. It was a hard winter. Everybody said so, and when Jap gazed at Ellis across the turnips and sorghum of those weary months, he said he believed it.

"Shame on you," rebuked Ellis, gulping his turnips with haste. "Think of the wretched people who would be glad to get this food."

"Do you know any of their addresses?" asked Jap abruptly. "Because I can't imagine anybody happy on turnips and sorghum. I'd be willin' to trade my wretched for theirn."

Kelly said that Jap would be fat as butter if he ate plenty of molasses, and this helped at first; but when the grass came, he begged Ellis to cook it for a change.

When George Thomas came in, one blustery March day, to say that if the turnips were all gone, he would bring in some more, Ellis pied Judge Bowers's speech on the duties of the Village Fathers to the alleys, when he saw the malignant look that Jap cast upon the cheery farmer.

Once a week Bill and Jap drew straws to determine which one should fare forth in quest of funds, and for the first time in his brief business career, Jap was glad the depressing task had fallen to him. "Pi" was likely to bring on an acute attack of mental indigestion, and the boy had learned to dread Ellis Hinton's infrequent but illuminating flame of wrath.

The catastrophe had been blotted out, the last stickful of type had been set and Bill had gone home to supper when Jap, leg-weary and discouraged, wandered into the office. Ellis looked up from the form he was adjusting.

"How did you ever pick out this town?" the boy complained, turning the result of his day's collection on the table.

Ellis turned from the bit of pine he was whittling, a makeshift depressingly familiar to the country editor. He scanned the meager assortment of coins with anxious eye. Jap's lower jaw dropped.

"I'll have to fire you if you haven't got enough to pay for the paper."

"Got enough for that," said Jap mournfully, "but not enough for meat."

"Didn't Loghman owe for his ad?" Ellis demanded. "Did you ask him for it?"

"Says you owe him more 'n he's willin' for you to owe," Jap ventured.

Ellis sighed.

"Meat's not healthy this damp weather," he suggested. "Cook something light."

"It'll be darned light," said Jap. "There's one tater."

"No bread?" asked Ellis.

"Give that scrap to the cat," Jap returned. "Doc Hall says she's done eat all the mice in town and if we don't feed her she'll be eatin' off'n the subscribers."

"Confound Doc Hall," stormed Ellis. "You take your orders from me. That bread, stewed with potato, would have made a dandy dish." He shook the form to settle it, and faced Jap.

"How did I come to pick this place?" he said slowly. "Well, Jap, it was the dirtiest deal a boy ever got. I had a little money after my father died. I wanted to invest it in a newspaper, somewhere in the West, where the world was honest and young. I had served my apprenticeship in a dingy, narrow little New England office, and I thought my lifework was cut out for me. I had big dreams, Jap. I saw myself a power in my town. With straw and mud I wanted to build a town of brick and stone. Dreams, dreams, Jap, dreams. Some day you may have them, too."

He let his lean form slowly down into a chair. Jap

braced himself against the table as the narrative continued:

"In Hartford I met Hallam, the man who started the Bloomtown *Herald*. I heard his flattering version. I inspected his subscription list and studied the columns of his paper, full of ads. I bought. The subs were deadheads, the ads—gratuitous, for my undoing. It was indeed straw and mud, and, lad, it has remained straw and mud." He leaned his head on his hand for a moment.

"That was the year after you were born, Jap. I was only twenty-one. For a year I was hopeful; then I dragged like a dead dog. You will be surprised when I tell you what brought me to life again. I tell you this, boy, so that you will never despise Opportunity, though she may wear blue calico, as mine did.

"It was one dark, cold day. No human face had come inside the office for a week. That was the period of my life when I learned how human a cat can be. We were starving, the cat and me, with the advantage in favor of the cat. She could eat vermin. I sat by the table, wondering the quickest way to get out of it. Yes, Jap, the first and, God help me, the only time that life was worthless. The door opened and a plump woman dressed in blue calico, a sunbonnet pushed back from her smiling face, entered."

To Jap, who listened with his heart in his throat, it seemed that Ellis was quoting perhaps a page from the memoirs he had written for the benefit of his townsmen. His deep, melodious voice fell into the rhythmic cadence of a reader, as he continued:

" 'Howdy, Mr. Editor,' she chirped. 'I've been keenin' for a long time to come in to see you. I think you are aprintin' the finest paper I ever seen. I brought you a mess of sassage and a passel of bones from the killin'. It's so cold, they'll keep a spell. And here's a dollar for next year's paper. I don't want to miss a number. I am areadin' it over and over. Seems like you are agoin' to make a real town out of Bloomtown,' and with a friendly pat on the arm, she was gone."

Ellis brushed the long hair from his brow, the strange modulation went out of his voice and the fire returned to his brown eyes as he said:

"Jap, I got up from that table and fell on my knees, and right there I determined that starvation nor cold nor any other enemy should rout me. Jap, I am going to make Bloomtown a real town yet. My boy, that blue calico lady was Mrs. Kelly Jones."

CHAPTER III

ELLIS scowled and kicked his stool absently with his heels.

"Will you explain where the colons and semicolons have emigrated to?" he asked Bill, with suppressed wrath.

"We was short of quads, and I whittled 'em off."

Ellis glared at Bill's ingenuous face.

"And what, pray, did you whittle to take their place?"

"Never had no call to use 'em," muttered Bill, chewing up the item he had just disposed of. "I can say all that I can think with commas and periods."

"Abraham Lincoln used colons and semicolons," said Ellis, shortly, "and I am setting his immortal speech. What am I going to do about it, my intelligent co-printer?"

Bill coughed violently as the wad of paper slipped down his throat.

"Try George Washington," he advised. "They didn't have so much trimmin's to their talk them days."

Jap shoved a chair against the door sill and flung the door ajar to cut off the blast of hot air that swept the office.

"Gee-whiz!" he complained, "I'm chokin' on the dust. However did they get 'Bloomtown' hitched on to this patch of dirt? There ain't a flower 'in a mile, 'ceptin' the half-dead sprigs the wimmin are acoaxin' against their will."

"When I came here," said Ellis, "the old settlers told me that whenever I wanted information I should hunt up Kelly Jones. There he goes now. Call him in."

But Kelly was coming anyway. He carried a mysterious basket and his sun-burned face was full of suppressed excitement.

"Wife allowed that you and Jap must be putty nigh starved," he chuckled, shifting the quid to his other cheek. "I reckon she knowed that Jap done the cookin' Wednesdays and Thu'sdays."

He lifted the clean white towel from the basket, disclosing a pound of yellow butter, a glass of jelly, a loaf of bread and two pies, fairly reeking aroma.

"Fu'st blackberries," asserted Kelly. "I ain't had a pie myself yet, and wife forbid me to take a bite o' yourn."

"God bless the wife of our countryman, Kelly Jones. May her shade never grow less," said Ellis fervently, stowing the basket away. "If Jap and Bill stick all the matter on the hooks before noon, they may have pie. Otherwise the Editor of the *Herald* exercises his prerogative and eats both pies."

"Kelly," asked Jap abruptly, "why did they call this

patch of dust 'Bloomtown'? Did they ever have even peppergrass growin' along its edges?"

Kelly settled himself comfortably in Ellis's chair and draped his long legs over the exchanges. Filling his mouth with Granger twist, he said:

" 'Twa'n't because of the blooms. Fact is, it never was 'bloom' in the fu'st place. Old man Blome owned this track of land—his name was Jerusalem Blome. Folks used to say Jerusalem Blown. Purty nice story there is about this town and Barton, why neither of 'em has got a railroad, and why Barton is bigger in money and sca'cer in folks."

Ellis put his stickful of type on the case resignedly. Bill and Jap deposited their weary frames on the door-step. The hot wind blew in their faces, laden with dust. The smell of dried grass was odorous.

"Looks like it mout blow up a rain," said Kelly, sniffing approvingly.

"Well, Kelly," declared Ellis, "you have tied the wheels of this machine. Deliver the goods you promised. We are not interested in rain."

"Humph!" ruminated Kelly, "it was this-a-way: Old man Blome bought this track about the time that Luellen Barton moved to her plantation. It mout 'a' been sooner; I ain't sure. Barton—leastways, what is Barton now—belonged to old Simpson Barton. When he went south and married a rip-snortin' widow, he brought his wife and a passel o' niggers to live at the old home place. There hadn't never been no niggers there, along of the fu'st Mis' Barton.

"When war broke out the niggers run away, along of Jerusalem Blome, that got up a nigger regimint. After the war there was talk of a railroad. It would run right through the Blome farm and cross the Barton place crossways. My daddy was overseer for Mis' Barton. Simp didn't have nothin' to say about the runnin' of the place. I was a tyke, doin' errands for everybody, and I heerd a lot o' the railroad talk. Old Blome was sellin' his farm in town lots, gettin' ready for the boom—for who would 'a' thought that Mis' Barton would turn her back on such a proposition?

"You see, it was this-a-way: Mis' Luellen was allus speculatin' in niggers, and a month before war broke, she had bought a load of Guinea niggers—the kind that looks like they are awearin' bustles, you know. Simp kinder smelt war, but, Lordee, Luellen wouldn't be dictated to! And she went broke, flat as a flitter. All that was left was the thousand acres of Barton land.

"Railroad? No, siree! She heard about old man Blome's activity, and she had it in for Blome. She sat up and primped her lips when Pee-Dee Jones come in behalf of the railroad. That's how the Barton Joneses come to settle in this neck o' the woods. Pee-Dee Jones —no kin o' mine—had a winnin' way, and he purty nigh got Mis' Luellen's name on the paper, when he let slip that he intended buildin' a town on her land. 'Do you think that I am agoin' to have a lot of blue-bellied Yankees in my very dooryard?' she yelled. 'You are mistaken.' And so she stuck.

"Afterwards she learned that Pee-Dee Jones had follered Grant. Whew! She nigh busted with rage. Mis' Luellen allus said that she could smell a Yankee a mile, and as she didn't like the smell, she cropped the railroad boom. It went five mile north of her place, and missed Bloomtown twenty mile. That's why the two towns are just livin' along. The folks that bought lots of old Blome tried to get another railroad to come their way. That was when the Wabash looked like it was headed for my farm; but I reckon that opportunities like that don't come but onct in a lifetime.

"I wonder that Mis' Luellen's spook don't howl around Barton every night, for Jones bought the big house after she died, and the fambly comes back there to live whenever their luck goes wrong. Pee-Dee's boy, Brons Jones, started a paper there, about the time that Hallam started the Bloomtown *Herald.* He sold out to a poor devil that's racin' to see if he can starve quicker'n Ellis. Brons ain't been around these parts, the last few years, but he owns a lot o' Barton property that he thinks 'll make good some day."

Kelly aimed a clear stream of tobacco juice at the dingy brown cuspidor, and made as if to settle himself for further narrative.

"Jap, Bill, get to work," commanded Ellis. "And,

Kelly, much as I appreciate you and your excellent wife, I must dispense with your society. I need these boys."

As the farmer departed, grinning cheerfully, Tom Granger appeared at the door of the *Herald* office. A conference of prominent citizens had been summoned to meet, early that afternoon, in the Granger and Harlow bank, a somewhat more pretentious building, separated from the *Herald* office by a narrow alley; and during a lull in the morning's business Tom was serving himself in the capacity of errand boy. From his place on the front steps, he could watch for the possible advent of depositor or daylight robber, there being no rear door to the bank.

"You'll be on hand, Ellis," he reminded. "Couldn't have any kind of a meeting without the *Herald*, you know. We won't keep you long."

But the session was more important than the banker had anticipated. Judge Bowers had prepared a lengthy discourse, and others had opinions that needed ventilating. Once or twice, Ellis was irritated by shrieks of laughter that emanated from the office across the alley, usually in Bill's shrill treble. When the cause of the merriment had reached an exceptional climax, the Editor pounced upon his assistants, wearing the scowl of a thunder god. Jap and Bill got up, shamefacedly, as he demanded:

"What do you think I am conducting this plant for? A circus for horse-play?"

He kicked the cat loose from the box Jap had it hitched to. The two boys looked ruefully at their over-turned cart.

"There goes the hell-box!" Bill screamed.

Ellis stared at him in transfixed wrath.

"Was that pi?" he demanded, looking down the hole in the floor into which most of the contents of the box had spilled.

Bill darted into the back room and sneaked swiftly out through the alley door. The office saw him no more that day. With such tools as were available, Jap set to work to undo the mischief he had wrought. An hour later, he replaced the plank in the floor. The rescued type was piled in a dirty litter of refuse. Ellis leaned over it, attracted by a gleam that shone as not even new type could glitter.

"It's a ring," explained Jap, furtively. "I reckon you won't be so mad now. I can soak it when we get hungry. I soaked my ma's ring, lots of times."

"Why, you young reprobate!" exclaimed Ellis, "that ring is not yours, or mine. We will advertise it." He smiled in Jap's disappointed face. "It looked like a beefsteak, didn't it, boy? Well, virtue is its own reward, and maybe the owner will pay for the ad."

But she did not, and yet the kick given to the inoffensive office cat had effects as far-reaching in the result to Bloomtown as did the kick of the famous Chicago cow, with this difference, that the effects were not disastrous. The brief ad in the *Herald* brought Flossy Bowers from her home in Barton to claim a ring she had lost fifteen years before.

"The office used to belong to Pap's daddy," Bill explained to Jap, as Ellis and Miss Bowers stood chatting in the front door. "When Grandpap was lawyerin', he had this for his office, and Aunt Flossy lost her ring, scrubbin' the floor. I have heard tell that he made the wimmin folks curry the horses. They say he had a big funeral. I wonder—" Bill spoke wistfully, "I wonder if I have any kinfolks on the man-side that love anybody but theirselves. Flossy didn't get to go off to school till her daddy died. She's been teachin', up to Barton, since my pappy married this last time, and my stepmother don't like her, so she never comes home."

Jap and Bill noted that Ellis found frequent business in Barton, and despite the inhospitable atmosphere of the substantial Bowers home, across the little park from the *Herald* office, Flossy came oftener than usual to her girlhood town. The autumn, the winter and the spring sped by. Ellis Hinton was too happy to scold, even when there was an excess of horse-play. In the gladsome June-tide the young girls of Bloomtown stripped their mothers' gardens to weave garlands for the little church, and Judge Bowers opened his heart and his house for the wedding reception.

Flossy had a dower of two thousand dollars, besides the cottage, a part of her father's patrimony, on one of the side streets, a ten-minute walk from the office. In her trunk were stowed away the yellow linens that should have served her, had a certain college friend proved faithful, and the wedding presents came near to doing the rest. This strange turn of the wheel of fortune landed Jap Herron in his first real home. Flossy could cook, and thank the kind fates, she brought something to cook with her. Flossy was a misnomer, for even in her salad days, she had never been the least bit "flossy," and when Ellis bestowed himself upon her she had well turned thirty.

The Judge made Ellis a present of the office, thereby relieving him of the haunting fear that he might, at some time, demand the rent. The paper put on a new dress, and the hell-box was dumped full of the discarded, mutilated types that had so long given strabismus to the patient readers of the Bloomtown *Herald*.

CHAPTER IV

"To-morrow is Jap's birthday," announced Ellis, one noontide early in July. "Jap, you are a joy-spoiler. With the Fourth yet smoking in the air, we must be upset by your birthday."

"Dad allus cussed that day," remarked Jap, wiping the blackberry juice from his freckled face. "Gee, I never guessed that there was such grub as this," regretfully gazing at the generous blackberry cobbler—regretfully, because his exhausted stomach refused to give another stitch.

"Cussed it?" queried Ellis, who was beginning to fat up a bit.

"He said that I was the first nail in the coffin of his troubles," replied Jap cheerfully.

"How dreadfully inhuman," exclaimed Flossy, scraping the scraps to the chickens. "Well, Jappie," she bustled back to the dining-room where her little family lingered, "we are going to begin making your birthdays pleasant. What do you want most?"

She had her mind's eye on the discarded ties of gorgeous hue, bought while Ellis was courting, and still brand new.

"Ca-can I have just what I want?" stuttered Jap, excitedly.

"Why, certainly, Jappie. That is, if we can afford it."

"Well—well," floundered Jap, astounded at his own temerity, "I allus wanted a pair of knee pants. Ma thought that some time she could get 'em; but the folks that she washed for allus kept giving her pants of their menfolks. I had to wear 'em. Can I have knee pants?"

Flossy stared dazedly after Ellis, whose vision of Jap in knee trousers was most unsettling. Before the momentous request had been granted, he was already half way down the alley. He was still convulsed with laughter when he reached the side door of the *Herald* office. But his mental picture paled into dull commonplace, by comparison with the reality that was in store for him.

Jap bought the cherished pants!

Bloomtown had seen the circus, the Methodist church fire and Judge Lester's funeral, the greatest in the history of the county; but none of these created the interest that Jap brought out when he traveled the length of Spring street, rounded the corner at Blanke's drug store and walked solemnly along Main street to the office.

Ellis was looking out of the window when he appeared, and despite his effort at composure, was writhing on the floor in agony when Jap entered. Bill looked up, as the vision crossed the threshold, and he involuntarily swallowed four type he was holding in his lips while he adjusted a pied stickful of "More Anon's" communication from Pluffot. Jap was so interested in himself that these things passed him by. He sat solemnly on his stool and looked vacantly into the e-box. Poking absently among the dusty types, he said, with profound solemnity:

"Bill, did you ever want anything right bad?"

Bill swallowed the last type with difficulty. It was the last capital Z, and they were getting five dollars for the announcement of Zachariah Zigler's daughter, Zella Zena's graduation into matrimony, and Bill had been picking enough Z's out of the "More Anon" to spell it, when the pi happened. His mind feebly recognized the calamity. He stared at the apparition before him, too stunned by the catastrophe to apprehend Jap's appearance further. Jap pressed him for reply.

"Once," he admitted gloomily. "I wanted to eat musherroons."

"Did you like 'em—when you got them?" asked Jap wanly.

"Naw! Tasted nasty. Never could see why folks keened after 'em."

Jap sighed.

"I allus wanted knee pants," he said plaintively. "But seems like I wa'n't made for that kind of luxury.

I ain't a bit happy, like I thought. Seems kind of indecent to show your legs, when you never done it before."

And Jap donned his long trousers again, much to the relief of Bloomtown. Ellis afterward declared that the three-and-a-half feet of spindling legs that dangled along under the buckled bands of those short trousers were the most remarkable things he had ever seen. They resembled nothing more than the legs of a spring lamb, cavorting in knee pants, in the butcher's window.

When we have achieved our heart's desire, we often taste the ashes of illusion.

Jap did not worry further about his appearance, but, dressed in the neat jumpers that Flossy provided, he seemed content. The memory of the episode was beginning to lose some of its sting when Dame Fortune gave a mighty turn to her wheel. He was in the alley with Bill, playing marbles, when Wat Harlow came rushing out.

"Where is Ellis?" he gasped. "There's hell afloat."

"Ellis and Flossy have gone to Birdtown to stay till Monday," vouchsafed Bill. "It's goin' to be big doin's at an anniversary, Sunday."

"Good God!" cried Wat, "what can I do?"

Jap arose and dusted himself.

"Is it a dark secret?" he inquired. "Did Ellis owe you a bill? Lordee, man, you can find plenty more in your fix. Forget it."

Wat continued to tear up and down the narrow alley.

"I'm ruined," he groaned. "They've got an infernal lie out about me, and it's going to kill me out."

Jap was interested.

"Maybe I know what Ellis could do," he suggested.

"I am running for the Legislature again," Wat said, pacing wildly over the marbles. "The Morgan crowd have got it out that I sold myself to the crowd that are trying to lobby a bill for a big appropriation for the State University. The county is solid against it, and they will vote me out of politics forever."

"What could Ellis do?" asked Jap, sympathetically.

"I thought that he could print the truth in handbills that could be sent out. It is now Friday, and Tuesday is election day. There will be no chance for help after Monday. They would have to have time to get all over the county." He sat down and wiped his forehead.

"What is your defense?" asked Jap judicially.

"They said that I was in the headquarters of the University gang—and I was," he said bitterly. "They said I shook hands with Barks—and I did. They said that he walked with me down the steps, with his arm around my shoulder—and he did."

"Love of Mike!" exploded Bill, "what do you want to talk about it for, then?"

"The University headquarters are in Bolton's furniture store," explained Wat. "My—my baby died last

night, and I went there for her little coffin." He choked
and walked over to the gate. After a moment he turned
back. "Barks was there. When he found why I came,
he walked out with me. He put his arm around my
shoulder. He—he was telling me that he buried his
youngest, a few weeks ago. And now, while I am tied
here, and the time is so short, Ellis is gone. And I'll
be ruined!"

He leaned heavily on the rickety gate. Bill wiped
his snub nose, openly, but Jap straightened up. The
fire of battle was in his eyes.

"Come inside," he cried valiantly. "Ellis is gone,
but the office is here. Come on, Bill. We have great
things to do."

All night long the two boys labored. After the story
was in type, they printed it on the Washington press.
It was Bill's suggestion that brought forth a can of
vermilion, to lend color to the heart story. Wat was
in and out all night, but there was no "in and out" for
the boys. At daybreak they flung the last handbill
upon the stack of bills and sank exhausted upon them.
Wat carried a mail pouch full of them to the stage
that started on its daily trip to Faber, at seven o'clock,
and the pathetic story saved the day for Legislator
Harlow.

"Boys, I will never forget it," he declared.

Ellis saw one of the badly spelled, ink-smeared
agonies on Saturday evening, and took the next stage

for home, wrathful enough to thrash both boys. They had adorned the bill with the cut that Ellis had had made for Johnson, the tombstone cutter, a weeping angel drooping its long wings over a stately head-stone. A rooster and two prancing stallions at the bottom presaged victory for the vilified Wat.

It was midnight when Ellis slammed the door open. The two boys were asleep in the midst of the litter of torn, ink-gaumed and otherwise spoiled copies of that hideous handbill. The last pull on the lever of the press had let it fly back too quickly, and it had flapped its handle loose and lay wrecked on the floor. The office had the appearance of a battleground. The ink was blood, and the press and scattered type, casualties. He stirred the boys with an angry kick. Jap sat up and peered through the ink over his eyes at his angry employer.

"We fixed him solid," he declared jubilantly. "There can't nothing beat Wat now. We opened the eyes of the county."

"You surely did," groaned Ellis. "When the Press Association add to their Hall of Fame, they will shroud me in the folds of that dad-blamed bit of art!"

CHAPTER V

Jap came running into the office, early in January, his freckled face aglow, his red hair standing wildly erect.

"Golly Haggins!" he exploded, "I got a letter from Wat. He's up at the Legislater and he writes—he writes this!" He fairly lunged the letter at Ellis.

Ellis read, scowling:

"My dear young Friend,—

"I am at the Halls of Justice and I want to fill my promise to reward you for the noble deed you done. There is a chance for a bright boy as page, and I have spoke for it for my noble boy. Come at once. Time and tide won't wait, and there is thirty other boys camped on the trail,

"Respectfully your Friend,
"Wat Harlow."

"Whoopee!" yelled Bill, jumping from his stool and turning a handspring across the office.

"Reckon I'd better ask Flossy to fix my things—get my clothes out?" asked Jap, beaming radiantly over the big barrel stove. He started toward the door.

"Stop!" said Ellis, in a voice Jap had never heard. "You are not going."

"Not going?" echoed both boys hollowly.

"No!" almost shouted Ellis, his brown eyes flashing. "I might have expected this from that wooden-headed son of a lost art. Do you think that you are going to leave my office to lick the boots of that loafing gang of pie-biters? Not in a thousand years! I am going to put a tuck in that idea right now. And while I'm talking about it, you may as well know that Flossy is getting ready to teach you how to 'read and write and 'rithmetic,' as Bill says. And as for you, Bill, Flossy says that if your father hasn't enough pride to do the right thing by you, she'll give you an education, along with Jap. You begin your lessons to-morrow evening.

"Jap, write to that reformed auctioneer and thank him for his favor. Tell him that you belong to the ancient and honorable order of printers. When he runs for governor, you will boom him. Till then, nothing doing in the 'Halls of Justice.'"

Jap sulked all day, but he wrote the letter whose contents might have changed his career, and the following evening he and Bill began the schooling that Flossy had planned. It was a full winter for the boys, the most important of their lives. Even when spring came, with its yawns and its drowsy fever, they begged that the lessons continue. Already the effect was beginning to show in the galley proof.

One morning in July, Jap had held down the office alone. Flossy was not well, and Ellis spent as much time with her as possible. Bill blustered in, a look of disgust in his brown eyes.

"Ain't nothin' doin' in town, 'cept at Summers's," he exploded, luxuriating in the kind of speech that was tabooed in the presence of his elders. "Only ad I could scare up was at Summers's, and Ellis don't want that."

Jap looked from the door, beyond the little village park and the hotel, to where the dingy white face of the saloon stared impudently upon the town.

"I never see one of them places without scringin'," he said slowly. "My pappy almost lived in one. When we were cold, he was warm. When Ma and us children were hungry, the saloon fed him, because—because he could be so amusing and entertaining when he was half drunk. Ma said that my pappy's folks were quality, but they didn't have any time for him.

"I used to creep around to the side winder to see what kind of a drunk he had. If it was a mean one, I'd run home and sneak Aggie out and hide. He had a spite agin us two, and when he had a mean drunk he used to beat us. He was skeered to tetch Fanny Maud. She had the wild-cattest temper you ever saw. He tried to pull her out of bed by her hair one night, and she jumped on him and scratched his face like a map. Ma had to drag her off, and if he hadn't run, Fanny would 'a' got him again. After that he would brag what a fine girl she was. One night Aggie and me hid in a straw stack all night."

Bill looked sorrowfully upon his friend.

"I thought I was the most forsakenest boy in the world," he said. "But my father never beat me, and he never touches no kind of licker. He just don't like me around. You know my mother died when I was born, and somehow he seems to blame it on me. I don't know how to figger it, for he married in a year, and when that one died it didn't take him no time to start lookin' out again. He hardly ever speaks to me, 'cept to cuss me or tell me what a nuisance I am. Allus makes me feel like a cabbage worm."

"Cabbage worm?" queried Jap.

"Yes, they turn green when they eat, and I feel like I am green, every bite I take. He looks at me so mean, like he thought I hadn't any right to eat. That's why I eat at Flossy's, every time she asks me. The only nice thing my pappy ever done for me was to put me in here with Ellis. Jap," he broke off suddenly, "I'm durn glad you licked me, that day. But your hair *was* red!"

Ellis had come quietly in at the rear door and had listened, half consciously, to the sacred confession. His face saddened for a moment. Then he squared his shoulders and his dark eyes flashed.

"I am going to make men of those boys yet," he promised himself. "Who knows——"

He interrupted the spasm of painful speculation, the dark foreboding that had for days hovered over him. The heat of summer and his anxiety over Flossy were beginning to tell on his nerves. He tiptoed softly out of the back door, across the weed-grown yard and out through the alley gate. A moment later he came in at the front door, whistling blithely.

The summer was intensely hot. As the dog-days waxed, Ellis grew ever more and more morose. His sharp bursts of temper were made tolerable only by the swift justice of the amend. Late in September he came down to the office one morning, pale and shaken. The boys had been sticking type for an hour when his sudden entrance startled them.

"Flossy is very sick," he said with lips that quivered, "and I will have to trust you boys."

Jap followed him to the door. His face was downcast.

"Is it true, Ellis? Bill said that Flossy would—would——" He gulped. He could not finish. Ellis turned suddenly and sat down at the table and buried his face in the pile of exchanges. His body shook with the effort to suppress his emotion. Bill slipped down from his stool and the two awkward, ungainly youths looked at each other in embarrassed sorrow. Finally Jap laid an inky hand on Ellis's shoulder.

"Tell her—tell her," he stuttered, "that Bill and me are—are a—prayin'."

Ellis gave a mighty sob and rushed away, bare-headed.

The two apprentices sat at their cases, the tears wetting the type in their sticks. The long day dragged by. Neither of them remembered noon, but plodded stolidly and silently through the clippings on their copy hooks.

It was growing dusk when a great commotion arose. It seemed to come from the corner near Blanke's drug store. It gathered force as it neared Granger's bank. Now it had reached the mouth of the alley that separated the bank from the *Herald* office. There was cheering and laughter. Jap's face hardened. He slung one leg to the floor. How dared any one cheer or laugh, when Flossy lay dying?

In another instant Ellis burst into the room. His dark locks were rumpled, his eyes wild and bright.

"Get out all the roosters—and the stallions, too!" he shouted. "Open a can of vermilion and, in long pica, double-lead it: 'It is a boy!' "

Jap let the other leg fall and dragged himself around. His mouth had fallen loose on its hinges. He sat down on the floor and gaped foolishly at Ellis.

"She's feeling fine," babbled Ellis, "and you and Bill are coming in the morning to see the boy." He rushed out again.

Jap looked at Bill, glued to the stool, holding in one paralyzed hand the inverted stick.

"Gee!" said Jap.

In the morning they tiptoed into Flossy's room. Very pale and weak was the energetic little woman who had taken the moulding of their destinies into her hands. She smiled gently and, as mothers have done since time was, she tenderly drew back the covers from a tiny black head and motioned for the two to look.

"Our boy," she said, smiling radiantly. "I am going to name him Jasper William, and I want you to make him very proud of the men he was named for."

The hot tears sprang to Jap's eyes and fell upon the little red face. The wee mite, perhaps prompted by an angel whisper from the land from whence he came, threw aloft one wrinkled hand and touched him on the cheek. Sobbing stormily, Jap hid his face in the covers as he knelt beside the bed. Then he took the little fingers in his.

"If God lets me live, Flossy, I will make him proud of me."

He choked and dashed outside to join Bill, who was snubbing audibly on the back steps. After a muffled silence he said, his eyes growing suddenly bright:

"Bill, did you notice what Flossy said? She said the men' that he was named after. Bill, we've got to quit kiddin' and begin to grow up."

CHAPTER VI

Time passed, after the easy-going manner of Bloom-town. Jap was sixteen, long, ungainly and stooped from bending over the case. Bill, a little older in months, but possessed of immortal youth, was stocky and rather good looking. Four years of daily inter-course had wrought a subtle change in their relations, four years of the stern and the sweet that Ellis and Flossy Hinton had brought, for the first time, into their lives.

Bill was at the table, the exchanges pushed back in a disorderly heap, as he surreptitiously figured a tough problem in bookkeeping that Flossy had given him. Jap, with furtive air, bolted the history lesson that ought to have been learned the day before. Ellis, his back to the one big window in the office, scowled over the proofs he was rattling. From time to time he pep-pered the air with remarks that fell like bird shot on the tough oblivion of his two assistants. At length for-bearance gave way under the strain, and he said, in cold and measured tones:

"When you are unable to decipher the idea I am trying to convey, I wish that you would take me into your confidence."

Bill looked up, a grin on his round, shining face, a grin that was fixed to immobility by the fierceness of Ellis's glance.

"I note that you have injected much native humor into perfectly legitimate prose," the stern voice continued. He read:

" 'Jim Blanke has a splendid assortment of sundays.' Now please explain. You are causing the good folks of this town unnecessary worry. My copy reads, 'sundries.' "

"Jap done it," vouchsafed Bill.

"Who *done* this?" Ellis stressed the verbal blunder witheringly, as he pointed his pencil at the next item. It read:

"Ross Hawkins soled twenty-five yearling calves."

"It looked that way," argued Jap.

"A devil of a couple you are," declared Ellis wrathfully. "Can't either of you reason? Did you ever hear of any one soling a yearling calf? Ross Hawkins is an auctioneer, not a shoemaker."

The boys looked sheepishly at each other. Suddenly Bill flung himself on his stomach and howled in glee.

"Lordee! What if that had 'a' got in the paper!" he gasped.

"There would be two fine, large, lazy boys out of a job," Ellis said severely.

He threw aside the copy and lifted the type. Jap

followed the movement with anxious eye. Another explosion hung, tense and imminent, in the air.

"Have you washed that type yet, Bill?" he asked, eager to placate Ellis.

It was the custom for the boy nearest the door to disappear when the time for washing a form was at hand.

"It was your job," protested Bill. "You promised to wash Wat Harlow's speech if I cleaned Kelly Jones's stock bill."

Ellis sat down wearily.

"Oh, we're agoing to do it all, this evening," cried Bill, defiantly. "You promised that we could clean out that box of cuts. You promised a long time ago."

"Go to it," said Ellis, his voice relaxing, and the two boys bolted into the back room. A little later he joined them. Jap and Bill sat on the floor, blowing the dust from a lot of dirty old woodcuts.

"I bought them with the job," he said, turning the pile over with his foot. He sat down on the emptied box and watched them as they examined the cuts.

"What is this?" asked Jap, peering at the largest block in the lot.

"That is a cut of the town, as it was when I came here," said Ellis, a shadow of reminiscence crossing his face, as he took the block in his long fingers.

Bill drew himself to his knees and looked at the maze

of lines and depressions curiously. The picture was as strange to him as it was to Jap. Ellis continued:

"There were three business houses here, besides the blacksmith shop and the saloon. Here they are. Ezra Bowers, Bill's grandfather, with the help of his three sons, ran a general store where they sold everything from castor oil to mowing machines. Phineas Blome— an unmistakable son of old Jerusalem—sold clothing and more castor oil and mowing machines. There wasn't such a thing as a butcher shop in Bloomtown. When the natives wanted fresh meat, they ordered it brought out on the hack. In other parts of the world, that institution is sometimes called a stage; but here I learned that its right name is 'hack.' The southern terminus of the Bloomtown, Barton and Faber hack-line, that has done its best for thirty years to prevent us from being entirely marooned, was over there at the south side of Blome's Park, exactly as it is to-day. The hotel didn't have a bit more paint, the first night I slept in it, than it has now."

"Flossy said that weathered shingles were fashionable," Bill grinned, taking up another cut. "Here's the Public Square—you call it Blome's Park, but I never heard anybody else call it that," he added, his voice lifting in a note of query. "That's the Square, all right, and the Town Hall, with 'leven horses hitched in front of it."

"Yes, when old man Blome laid out his farm in town

lots, he reserved his woods pasture for a city park.
You never heard of an orthodox town that didn't begin
with a Public Square, and that little rocky glade with
the wet-weather spring had the only trees within ten
miles of here. It wasn't fit for farming, so Blome
argued that nobody would buy it with a view to raising
garden truck. But your foxy Uncle Blome didn't sacrifice anything by his generosity to the town that was
about to be born. He reserved the lots facing the park
on three sides, and held them at an exorbitant figure—
as much as five dollars a front foot, I should say.

"The lots at the north and east were to be sold for
high-class residences only. Those at the west were
reserved for business houses. Behold the embryo Main
street! Overlooking the park at the south was Blome's
farm house, since metamorphosed into a tavern and
barns for the stage horses. The last of the Blomes
shook the dust of Bloomtown from his feet when Carter
bought his interest in the hack line. Bill's grandfather
had a farm adjoining Blome's land at the west; but
Ezra Bowers, merchant prince and attorney-at-law,"
he said whimsically, "had to have a residence in the
fashionable quarter, fronting the park. A little patch
of the old farm is quite good enough for Mr. and Mrs.
Ellis Hinton and their two sons, Jap and Jasper William."

Jap caught Ellis's hand, a lump arising in his throat.
Bill relieved the momentary tension by turning over

another cut. A familiar face looked out at him from the grime of years. Ellis glanced at it and smiled.

"It is a great thing, Jap, the birth of a town. Bloomtown was really never born. The stork dropped her when he was traveling for a friendly haven. For ten years she lay, just as she fell, without visible signs of life. About twenty families existed, somehow. They had pigs, chickens and garden truck, and to all intents they would go on existing till the last trump.

"One day I went out into the country to attend a sale. Boys, I was never so well pleased with a day's work as I was with that day's jaunt. I heard the most masterly bit of eloquence that ever came from the lips of an auctioneer. The man had the crowd hypnotized. He even sold me an accordion, a thing I was born to hate. The fact that it was wind-broken and rattly never occurred to me until I woke up, after he had done. Then I went to him and said:

"'You an auctioneer! You should be in the Halls of Justice, telling the people how to interpret their laws.'

"The idea struck him. He came into town with me and we talked the matter over. He was easily the best known and most liked man in the county. It was then that the political bug stung our good friend, Wat Harlow. Wat moved his family to town and soon he had a decent habitation. He stimulated a rain of paint and a hail of shingle nails. He prodded the older inhabitants to an era of wooden pavements and stone crossings. Bill's grandfather objected, because he said it cut down the sale of rubber hip-boots; but Wat's eloquence was the key to fit anything that tried to lock the wheels of progress. He did more than that. He brought Jim Blanke from Leesburg to start a decent drug store.

"After that he robbed Barton of Tom Granger, and together they started the first bank of Bloomtown. Granger's wife and baby, with Wat's wife, were the civilization. Mrs. Granger was almost an invalid, even then, but she gathered the women together and formed an aid society. She begged and cajoled Bowers out of enough money to build a little church on the lot that Blome had donated. I joined the church, for the moral example. I don't remember what denomination it was supposed to be. We had services once a month; but Mrs. Granger was the real power in the town. She introduced boiled shirts and neckties. Tom bought the big patch of ground, north of the park, and set out those elm trees before his foundation was in. Then Jim Blanke got Otto Kraus to come here and start a private school. Otto played the little cabinet organ in church, and taught all the children music, after school hours. Thus was Bloomtown born. Wat Harlow made the blood circulate in her moribund veins."

Jap looked into Ellis's face, his freckled cheeks glowing.

"That's not what Wat Harlow said," he declared breathlessly.

"What did he say?" asked Ellis sharply.

"Why—why," gulped Jap, "he said that Bloomtown was dead as a herring, and too no-account to be buried, till Ellis Hinton came and jerked her out of the mud and started her to breathe."

Ellis got up and dusted his trousers.

"As I said before, Wat was an eloquent auctioneer. Talk is his trade, and he keeps in practice. Dilute his enthusiasm one-half, Jap. And now, get to work, washing up."

As he left the office he encountered a group of tittering girls, in front of the bank. They scattered when they perceived that Ellis and not Bill had come forth. Bill was the lion of the town. Already the girls had begun to come after papa's paper, on publishing day, which upset the machinery of the office, never too dependable.

One Thursday when the air was full of snow, the little office registered its capacity crowd. Ellis was at home with a heavy cold, and Jap and Bill were getting out the paper. The ink congealed on the rollers and needed constant warming to lubricate the items reposing on the bosom of the Washington press. This warming was Bill's job, and Jap was exasperated to fighting pitch by the dilatory method of Bill's peregrinations around the circle of rosy-faced girls, hanging admiringly on his efforts.

"Chase those girls out," he growled. "No use for them to hang around. We won't get this paper out in a week if they stick around after you."

"Old Crabby!" sniffed one of the girls. "You're just mad because nobody wants to hang after you."

"Jap is particular," chaffed Bill, half apologetically. Since they had assumed the responsibility for the right uplift of Flossy's boy, there had been growing a new, shy pride in themselves. "Better wait and come back in the morning," he suggested.

The girls filed slowly out. As they passed the table, where Jap was piling the papers to fold, Isabel Granger, doubtless inspired by the demon of mischief, leaned forward suddenly and kissed him full on the mouth. Then she fled, shrieking with glee. Jap stood as if stricken to stone. Bill looked at him in fright. There was no color in his freckled face. His gray eyes were staring, as if some wonderful vision had blasted his sight.

"Gee, Jap," said Bill uneasily, "are you sick?"

Jap aroused himself and turned toward the press.

"No," he said slowly, "but I don't like for folks to be familiar like that. If I wanted to be a fool like you——" He stopped and stared a moment from the window.

"The next time she kisses me," he said shortly, "she will mean it."

CHAPTER VII

WHAT a wonderful thing is a baby! Babies were not new to either Bill or Jap. In Bill's memory lingered the shrill duet of his twin half-sisters, a continuous performance that had lasted more than a year. And Jap had never fully corrected a lurch to the left side, due to carrying his sister, Agnesia, when he was little more than a baby himself. Yet the little visitor from the Land of Yesterday was a never failing miracle to them. His cry filled them with fear for his well-being, and his laugh intoxicated them with its glee.

"Wait till he can talk," smiled Flossy. "Then you will see how wise he is."

In her heart she was beginning to combat the fear that he would never talk. Other children of his age were already chattering like magpies.

"Ma said that I said 'papa' when I was eight months old," declared Jap. "But I don't know why I should 'a' said that."

Bill grinned fatuously as the baby pulled at his hair.

"Bill won't get his hair cut," said Jap. "He knows that J. W. would hang after me, if it wasn't for his curly hair."

The little fellow, who for obvious reasons could be neither Jasper nor William, had learned to respond with amiable toleration to the soothing abbreviation, "J. W." Kicking his stubby legs gleefully, he tangled his fingers more mercilessly in Bill's brown locks. Flossy loosed the fingers gently, as she cooed:

"Naughty, naughty! Mamma said baby mustn't."

Flinging his fingers aloft in protest, he gurgled:

"Ja—Bi!"

Flossy's eyes shone with sudden joy. It was her son's first attempt at articulate speech. The boys lunged forward with one impulse.

"He said 'Jappie,'" Jap cried, his chest swelling with the importance of it. Bill glared.

"Why, Jap!" Pain and indignation were in his tone. "He tried to say 'Bill.'"

Flossy smiled on them both. It was a wonderful little kingdom, of which she had assumed the place of absolute monarch, a monarch so gentle and so just that her sway was never questioned.

"Ellis puts in half his time trying to teach baby to say the two names all in one mouthful, so that you boys won't fight about his first word," she vouchsafed. "It would have to be either Jap or Bill, because you never tell him anything but your names."

When they waved their caps in farewell, they were still discussing the mooted question vehemently. Was it "Jappie," or a combination of Jap and Bill? To

both of them the question was vital. Jap had the better of the argument, when Bill blurted:

"Anyhow, he's my cousin, and he ain't no relation of
yours." Then he remembered that significant remark
of Ellis's: "A little patch of the old farm is quite good
enough for Mr. and Mrs. Ellis Hinton and their two
sons, Jap and Jasper William," and he was silent the
rest of the way back to the office.

Little J. W. was three years old before he could
speak distinctly. The child was born with other af-
flictions than the serious impediment to his speech, and
the four who hung with anguished love on his every
gesture were never free from a certain unnamed anxiety.
He loved Bill, but he worshipped Jap. Both were his
willing slaves.

One rainy, dismal night in early fall, when Bill's stepmother lay seriously ill, Flossy left her baby to the care
of the small but usually capable maid who assisted her
with the work of the cottage, while she and Ellis went
to the home of Judge Bowers to relieve the trained
nurse who had come up from the city. At the supper
table, Ellis had remarked that Jap and Bill would be
working late that night, in order to get out a job that
had come in when all the resources of the office were
needed for the weekly edition of the *Herald*. He had
added that he would go over and help them, if his presence could be spared from the sick-room.

The remark must have lodged in the baby's mind,

for he slipped out of bed, while the maid was employed in the kitchen, and toddled through the cold rain almost all the way to Main street. Jim Blanke found him lying exhausted in the road, a little way from the drug store, the rain beating pitilessly on his unconscious head and his scantily clad body.

After a night of anxious care, the little fellow relapsed into a state of coma, and lay for hours, white and still, save for the rasping of his breath. The office was closed. Both boys, frantic with fear, stood with Ellis as the child lay in his mother's arms, the four dreading that each hoarse breath would be his last. Flossy sat erect in the wide rocking chair, her brave eyes watching every sigh that tore the little bosom. Dr. Hall, whose dictum was life and death, was silent. And this silence was the last straw for Jap. He crept nearer. In fear, he turned from the face of the beloved sufferer. Ellis caught the look in the boy's anguished eyes, and a spasm crossed his tightly compressed lips. The physician rallied himself from the torpor of despair that had laid hold on him.

"Try to arouse him," he commanded. "Try again." The resources of his experience and his prescription blank had long since been exhausted.

Flossy bent over her child and called softly:

"Baby, dearest, mamma loves you. Won't you speak?"

Ellis leaned forward. His face blanched. The rasping had ceased! Jap caught the look of horror, and dragged himself up to look into the baby's face.

"He isn't dead! He's all right!" he shrieked, not knowing that he spoke. "He's still breathing. I can hear him." His hands grasped the cold body and lifted it, unconscious of the thing he was doing.

"Oh, J. W.! Oh, J. W.!" he screamed, "don't go away from us!"

He pressed the child to his breast convulsively, and the miracle happened. The solemn black eyes opened and a husky voice said, "Jappie."

After the excitement was over, and the exhausted mother slept beside her sleeping child, Bill said humbly:

"He did say 'Jap' first."

"But he tried to say 'Bill,' too," Jap said loyally.

The next morning, when the office had resumed its normal routine, a routine that was destined to be only partially interrupted by the death of Bill's second stepmother, a few days later, Ellis called Jap into the little back room where, in the dismal days before Flossy's coming, they had performed all the functions of housekeeping. He closed the door, as he laid his hand on Jap's shoulders.

"You saved J. W.'s life," he said solemnly. "Doc Hall said that you stopped him, on the threshold, when you gave that dreadful cry."

The baby did not rally, and Ellis worried about this incessantly. One day, some weeks after another mound had been added to the group in Judge Bowers's family lot, and Bill had gone with his father to appraise the merits of a prospective housekeeper from Birdtown, Ellis looked up from the proof he was correcting. Jap noted the anxiety in his face, and the gray eyes, that could so often render speech unnecessary, put the question. Ellis sighed.

"He's not getting along the way he ought to," he mused. "Doc Hall prescribed a tonic for him a month ago; but it doesn't seem to take hold. He has no constitution to begin with. His father, exhausted by privation and ill-health, has handicapped him in the start.

"Jap," he said, as he arose and laid one arm confidingly around the boy's shoulder, "you must remember that, in the years to come. I didn't give the baby a fair chance. He may need all the help he can get to carry him through. If you should live longer than I, you must be his father and big brother, both."

Jap's gray eyes opened in astonishment. The idea that there could ever be a time when Ellis would not be there had never entered his mind. He looked into the dark, thin face with its pallor and its unnaturally bright eyes, and a joyous smile took the place of the momentary shock.

"Doc Hall said that you had grit enough to outlive any disease that ever lurked in the brush of Bloomtown," he declared eagerly.

"Doc Hall is an optimist," Ellis laughed hollowly. "I'm not so much concerned for myself as for the boy and his mother. You know what J. W. means to her."

"Bill and I have already talked it over," Jap returned. "We're going to be big brothers to J. W. We're going to take turns at taking him for long rides on Judge Bowers's old horse, Jeremiah. Doc Hall said that long, jolty rides would set him up, rosy and fat, in a little while. Bill told me this morning that he had J. W. weighed again, on Hollins's scales, and he has gained three pounds."

Ellis Hinton's face cleared. There was a new elasticity in his step as he crossed the room and laid the copy down on the case. Unconsciously he began to whistle, as he clicked the type in the stick.

CHAPTER VIII

FLOSSY came into the office, leading the boy by the hand, and called Ellis aside. Old Jeremiah had done wonders for the little fellow; but on Flossy Hinton's face there was a look that boded ill to some one.

"I sent for Brother William to meet me here," she said crisply. "I want you to back up all that I say."

Before Ellis had breathed twice, she was out looking up the street, and in less time than you could think it out, she was back, towing the Judge, who puffed explosively. Ellis and the three boys had retreated to the rear office.

"There is not a bit of use to argue, William," she said, her lips in a hard, straight line. "Ellis has done more than any one else in town could do. When I heard that you had subscribed five thousand dollars to the new church, I concluded that your charity was a little far fetched. Now I want you to subscribe five thousand dollars to the institution that is making a man of your son. I want five thousand dollars for the printing office. It is too small, and the press is out of date. We need all that goes into an up-to-date printing office."

Her brother looked upon her tolerantly.

"Keep it up, Floss. It never fazed you to ask favors, and you ain't run down yet."

"It's a shame," she stormed. "Just look at this little shed! Why, even a cross-road blacksmith shop is better."

He looked around appraisingly.

"I reckon it'll house all Ellis's business," he commented.

"Ellis," she flashed, "tell William about the railroad."

Ellis came from the inside office. He generally withdrew from the conferences between Flossy and her brother.

"Wat Harlow told me that two of the big railroad systems have entered into a joint arrangement to shorten their mileage, on through trains to the West. He's got it all fixed for the new track to pass through Bloomtown. It will give us all the benefit of two railroads."

"You see," said Flossy triumphantly, "the town will boom. People will move in, and a first-class newspaper will be the greatest asset."

"I think that the town will take a big start," assured Ellis. "The boys will have all they can do with job work, and the office is small for our present needs."

"Pap, you should watch us carving letters when we get short," interposed Bill. "Last week Jap had to carve three A's for Allen's handbill. There are only three of 'em in that case, and Allen wanted to use six. His name is Pawhattan Abram Allen, and he wanted the whole blamed thing spelled out in caps. I told Jap it was lucky Allen's folks didn't name him Aaron, on top of all the rest."

"That's good practice for you boys," the Judge snorted. "I'm mighty glad you learned something for all the money I spent on you." He glanced at his sister witheringly; but Flossy had her eyes fixed on her husband.

"I wish," Ellis stirred himself to say, "that the town would boom enough to take all these frame shacks off of Main street, so that the place wouldn't look like a settlement of campers."

"A good fire would help," commented Bill boldly.

Judge Bowers looked over his glasses at his son.

"Well, when the railroad comes, and the rest of the shacks are moved out, I will write you a check for five thousand dollars," he snorted, turning his rotund form out of the door.

Flossy picked up the boy and flounced out, in speechless indignation. By argument and cajolery she had succeeded in getting six months apiece for Bill and Jap at the School of Journalism, and at twenty the boys were far more expert than Ellis was when he began the publication of the *Herald*. She had set her heart on the new printing office, and her eyes were abrim with tears as she stumbled home.

The week wore on until printing day. It was a day of unimagined exasperations. Everything went wrong. Ellis's usually smooth temper bent under the stormy comments of the boys, and in the late afternoon he developed a violent headache and went home. Things continued to pile up until it was evident that the boys would have to print the paper after dark.

It was ten o'clock when they finished. Jap followed Bill to the pavement, pausing to lock the door and slip the key in his pocket. The town was asleep. Not a soul was to be seen on Main street. Bill, who usually took the short cut across the Public Square to his father's house, turned with Jap and walked along Main street to the farther end of the block. At Blanke's drug store, he turned into Spring street. He was saying, in a tone of mixed penitence and anxiety:

"I wish we hadn't riled Ellis so, to-day. I don't like those headaches he's having so often, and the way his face gets red every afternoon. If he ever sneaked out and took a drink—But I know he never does."

"Oh, Ellis is all right, now that little J. W. is getting strong," Jap insisted.

They had gone some distance in the direction of Flossy's cottage, when Bill looked across an expanse of vacant lots to where a dim light burned in the loft of Bolton's barn.

"They're running a poker game," said Bill wisely.

Almost before the words were gone, a wild shriek rent

the air. A flash of light from the barn loft, a scrambling of feet, and a succession of dark objects catapulted the ooze of the barnyard, and it was all ablaze. A stiff breeze was blowing from the southwest. Bill ran to the mill to set the fire whistle, and Jap scrambled through a window of the Methodist church and began to fling the chimes abroad, so that he who slept might know that there was a fire in town. There had been no rain for weeks, and the frame structures were ripe for burning.

In less than half an hour the row of stores on Main street, in the block below the *Herald* office, began to smoke. From Hollins's grocery store a brand was carried by the wind and lodged among the dry shingles of Summers's saloon. The excitement was augmented, a few minutes later, by a series of pyrotechnic explosions. Bucket brigades were formed, the firemen mostly in undress uniform.

Jap and Bill were in their glory. Jap was mounted on top of the Town Hall, directing operations. Right down the row rushed the flames, eating up the town. As if in parting salutation, the fiery monster leaped across a vacant lot, thick set with dried weeds, and clutched with heat-red claws at the *Herald* office.

"This way, men!" yelled Jap. "You have to get the press and enough type out to tell about the fire."

Ellis was staring hopelessly at the flame that was licking at the rear of the office. The water was exhausted from the town well, and there was no hope of saving the plant. But youth is omniscient, and the townsmen followed the wildly yelling apprentices and hastened to demolish the office and drag away the debris, some of it already blazing. From the salvage rescued from Price's hardware store, and heaped in a disorderly pile in the Public Square, Jap handed out the latest thing in fire fighting apparatus. The flimsy structure, that had been Ellis Hinton's stronghold for almost twenty years, gave way to an assault with axes, and the contents, pretty well scattered, were left standing. It was nothing that Granger and Harlow's bank went down with little left to show its location save the fire-proof vault, and that only a shift in the wind prevented the flames from crossing to the fashionable residence section east of Main street.

In the morning the *Herald* force began business in the ruins of its time-worn shelter, and set up gory accounts of the fire, on brown manila paper with vermilion and black ink. A crowd assembled to watch the exciting spectacle.

"What's the use of a railroad now?" bleated Judge Bowers. "There ain't no town to run it through."

"Why ain't there?" asked Jap sharply.

"Why, all the folks are talking of pulling up stakes and moving to Barton."

"Well, if that is the kind of backbone they have been backing this town with," snapped the youth, his red hair standing erect, "you help them move, and the *Herald* will show them up for quitters—and fill the town with real men."

And being full of wrath, he proceeded to incorporate this thought in the half column he was setting up. The paper was eagerly snapped up by the crowd.

"Who wrote this?" fairly howled Tom Granger. "I want to hold his grimy hand and help him shout for a bigger and better town."

Ellis shoved Jap forward.

"Here is the fire-eater," he announced. Jap flushed through the dirt on his face.

"It's true," he said, half shyly. "There's no good in a quitter. The best thing is to smoke them out and get live men to take their places."

"Bravely said," shouted Granger. "The bank will rebuild with brick. Who else builds on Main street?"

Before the end of the following week the town was humming with industry. Every hack brought its contingent of insurance adjusters, and merchants elbowed contractors in the little telegraph office, in endeavors to get supplies. On Thursday a curious crowd stood watching Ellis and the boys run the blistered but still faithful Washington press in the boiling sun.

"Goin' to get winter after a while, Jap," shouted one of the bystanders. "You'll have to wear ear muffs to get out your paper."

Jap grinned and swung the lever around methodically.

"What are you going to do, Ellis?" asked the honorable member from the "Halls of Justice," who had hurried to his little home town in her hour of trouble. "There ain't a vacant shack in town. It seems a darned shame that you'll have to give up, after starving with the town till it gets its toes set in gravel at last. Now that the railroad is running this way like a scared wolf, the town needs a paper worse than ever."

"Who said they was going to quit?" demanded Judge Bowers pugnaciously. "They ain't! Ellis is goin' to have a two-story brick, with a printin' press that runs itself. This here town ain't no quitter." He glared fiercely at Harlow.

Jap lingered with Ellis until the last of the day's work was finished. As he started for home he came upon an animated group, in the shade of the half-burned drug store. Behind a pile of wreckage, Bill was holding court. Jap stopped short. Bill was telling a lurid tale of superhuman strength and dare-devil bravery, of which Jap Herron was the hero, a tale that grew with every telling. A wave of embarrassment swept over Jap. As he turned hastily away, he felt a soft clutch on his arm. He looked back. Two sparkling black eyes were looking up into his.

"I think that you are the bravest boy in the world,"

whispered Isabel Granger, "and—and I am glad I kissed you that time."

Jap stared at her, stunned by a new emotion. In another moment she was gone, flying across the street in the direction of her home.

"Anybody but Jap would 'a took her up on that," insinuated Bill, who had heard Isabel's last words.

Jap turned a murderous look upon him. The crowd of girls tittered as they dispersed. When supper was over Jap returned to the spot, and long after dark he sat upon the pile of wreckage, thinking long, long thoughts.

CHAPTER IX

The scraping of saw, the clang of hammer and the smell of fresh paint classed Bloomtown as "Boomtown." The railroad had already peered into the northern environs of the town, cutting diagonally across Main street, some half-dozen blocks from the plot of ground that had been rechristened Court House Square. A substantial municipal building took the place of the dingy old Town Hall, and the barns of the now almost defunct Bloomtown, Barton and Faber hack line had been cleared away to make room for a decent hotel. In the angle between the railroad tracks and Main street a small temporary station sheltered travelers. The half-moribund village had burst its swaddling bands and begun to expand. Everybody was wearing grins as a radiant garment.

As the summer traveled toward July, the headaches that had been so frequent the past winter merged into a feeling of utter exhaustion, and Ellis came down to the office but few days of each week. Flossy stopped Jap at the gate one noon hour.

"Ellis has something to tell you, Jappie, and I want you to be very composed. Don't let yourself go." Her voice was full of pleading. She turned quickly as Ellis appeared in the doorway. He walked out to meet them.

"Let us sit out under the trellis while Flossy finishes fixing dinner," he said, leading the way. "Jap, your birthday comes to-morrow, and I am going to ask you to accept a sacred trust that is a burden. You are twenty-one and, as they say, 'your own man.' I want to ask you to be *my man*. Jap, I am going away, how far God only knows. The doctor says that my lungs are all wrong, and life in the mountains may save me. My boy—for you have been my boy since you walked through my door, nine years ago—I want you to take charge of the office, and shoulder the support of Flossy and the little one if—if——" He caught the horror-stricken boy's hand. "Jap, I will never come back. I know it. I have talked with my soul and it is well. Will you do it, Jap?"

Jap pressed Ellis's feverish hand between his strong young palms. He could not speak. His eyes were dry and his lips twitched.

"There," cautioned Ellis, "no heavy face before Flossy. God bless her! she thinks that I will be well before the new office is done, and is making more splendid plans for the big opening! She is—— Jap, you dunce, grin about something!"

Flossy and the boy came dancing down the sun-

flecked path and Jap swung the slender little fellow to
his shoulder and began a mock race from Ellis.

As soon as dinner was over, a dinner that stuck in his
throat for hours, he told Flossy that two men were
rushing Bill to desperation for their handbills. He
hurried out by way of the alley. Flossy ran after him.

"You forgot your hat, Jap," she cried breathlessly.

He took the hat and started off silently.

"Wait a minute, Jap." Her voice was insistent.
"You didn't put on a grave face with Ellis, did you?
Oh, Jap"—the cry was from her heart—"he will never
live to see the new office! He will never know of the
realization of his dreams, the big town, the trains whirling through, and he looking down from his lofty window with a smile of superior joy. Oh, Jap, how often
have we heard him tell about it! He doesn't know.
He is full of hope. Only just before you came he was
joking about the Star Spangled Banner he was going
to wind around his brow when he dedicated the *Herald*
office. Jap, be true to his faith, for he will never open
the door of that office. He will never help to get out
the first paper."

She strangled and turned away. Then in brisk tones
she added:

"Now, Jap, hurry along. Here comes Ellis to scold."
And in the marvelous manner that is God-given to loving women, she forced a smile to her lips as she gave

the youth a playful shove and ran to meet her husband.

A few days later they left. The town took a holiday, and with laughter and merrymaking it celebrated Ellis Hinton's first vacation. A water tank was in process of construction, at the upper end of a half-mile stretch of double track, and at the lower end of the siding, close to Main street, the imposing brick railroad station stood in potential grandeur, its bricks still separated by straw and its ample foundation giving promise of stability as it reposed in sacks of cement and piles of crushed stone. Something of this was incorporated in Ellis's farewell speech as he addressed his townspeople. When the train began to move his black head was still visible, as he returned quip for joke. And Flossy was flitting from her lifelong friends as if no trouble clouded her brow.

Little J. W. was the feature of the going, and under the pretense of caring for his wants, their sleeper compartment had been piled with fruit and flowers by loving friends who had gone on to the nearest town to meet the train, so that the surprise should be the more complete. Then, to the sound of the village band, Ellis left what he had always called "my town." Jap did not go to the station, and when Bill found the door of their improvised office locked, he turned silently away. His heart was full, too.

The Widow Raymond had offered them a room for

a printing office. The press occupied the room. Jap and Bill set the type in the woodshed and carried the galleys in. During the nine years of their association Bill had been the unsteady member of the team, consuming more effort in devising ways and means of escaping work than the work would have cost, and toiling with feverish penitence when he realized that he had wrought a hardship to Jap or Ellis. But now, inspired by the dimpled face of Rosy Raymond, he worked as he had never worked in his life. Odd things began to happen. Bill insisted on doing all the proof-reading, a task he had hitherto detested. A bit of verse occasionally crept into the columns of the *Herald*. Jap did not detect this verse for several weeks. When he did, he descended upon Bill.

"Where in Heck did you filch that doggerel?"

"Who said it was doggerel?" demanded Bill.

"Lord love you," cried Jap, "what could any sane being call it? What did you get for publishing it—advertising rates?"

"You're a fool!" snapped Bill. "You think that you're a criterion. I will have you know that lots of folks have complimented it."

Jap took up the offending sheet.

" 'Thine eyes are blue, thine lips are red, thine locks are gold,' " he groaned. He looked at Bill. Just then the door opened and Rosy stepped into the room. A great light shone on Jap's understanding. Her eyes were blue, her lips certainly red, and a fervid imagination could call her hair gold. He sighed pathetically.

"Bill, don't you think you could write it out and relieve the pressure on your heart, without endangering our prestige?"

Bill kicked at the mongrel dog that had its habitat under the press, and marched out indignantly.

"I'll be glad if I get him out of here single," mused Jap. "He has these spells as regular as the seasons change. Heretofore his prospects have never entitled him to consideration. This time it may be different."

Bill had been systematically chased from every front gate in town, behind which rosy-cheeked girls abode; but the disquieting conviction swooped down upon Jap that Barkis, in the shape of the Widow Raymond, might be more than "willin'" to hitch Bill to her sixteen-year-old daughter. And if Bill had not contracted a new variety of measles at the most opportune time, Jap's forebodings might have been realized. Bill had the "catching" habit. No contagion in town ever escaped him, and this time he was so ill that he had to go to the country to recuperate.

The new stores opened, one by one, with much celebration. Owing to several unaccountable financial complications, the last of all the important buildings on Main street to be finished was the *Herald* office. A cylinder press, second-handed, to be sure, but none the less an object of admiration, was installed, and fonts of clean, new type stood ready for work. There was a great, sunny front office on the main floor, and the ample space behind it had been divided into composing room, press room and private office. On the second floor was a small job press, and here, at Jap's suggestion, the old Washington press was stored. The rooms were decorated with flags, and bunting was strung across the front of the office. Judge Bowers had personally attended to this.

"You're going to have a dandy paper," Tom Granger beamed, as he accompanied Jap on the final tour of inspection. "We'll all have to stop business to watch this cylinder press spill out the news."

Wat Harlow had run down from the Capital to congratulate the staff. At his suggestion the merchants had ordered flowers from the city, and great vases of roses and carnations, and decorative pieces in symbolic design, stood around in fragrant profusion. Every room of the office was filled with them.

The forms were ready for the printing of that first paper, and only awaited the conclusion of Wat's speech, to be placed upon the press, so that Bloomtown should receive the salutatory *Herald*. Jap turned to the assemblage, waiting in eager curiosity to see the cylinder revolve.

"The paper will be printed on Ellis's press," he said briefly. "I don't want to be ungrateful for your kindness, but will you leave Bill and me alone to get out our first edition?"

They filed out slowly, awed by the grief in the voice of Ellis's boy.

With the old types, on the old Washington hand press, they printed the first *Herald* of the new régime. With the exception of the greeting on the front page, every word was reprinted from the predictions written by Ellis in the years agone, and the greeting, in long pica on the first page, was his telegram to them and his townsmen received that morning.

When the last paper was printed by the two sad-faced boys on their day of jubilee, and the pile had been folded and carried downstairs, Jap closed the press upon the inky type, and gathered the great bunches of fragrant blossoms and heaped them upon the press, to be forever silent. With a groan of anguish, he threw himself against them. Bill slipped his arm through Jap's, and together they celebrated the day that was Ellis's. And in the night the telegram came:

"At rest. FLOSSY."

CHAPTER X

WHEN Ellis went away it was to the sound of jollity. He came back to a town shrouded in mourning. Every store was closed, and symbols of grief adorned most of them. Wat Harlow, with a delicacy Ellis would scarcely have expected of him, had ordered purple ribbon and white flowers to tie with the crape. Silent and griefstricken, the town stood waiting the arrival of the train. When it came, the coffin was lifted by loving hands and carried the ten long blocks to the church. No cold hearse rattled his precious body, but, even as the body of Robert Louis Stevenson was held by human touch until the last office was done, so was Ellis Hinton, the country printer, carried to his last repose by the hands of his friends.

Not until Jap looked for a long, anguished moment upon the flower-massed grave did he realize that he was alone, that he was drifting, that he had no anchor. Something of this he expressed to Flossy, between dry sobs, when they had left Ellis alone in the secluded little cemetery. Her eyes burned with a strange, maternal light as she comforted the boy whose grief was of the fibre of her own.

"Ellis knew that you would feel that way," she said
gently, "and because of that, he made a will that is to
be read to-night. Wat Harlow has it. Until it is read,
I want you not to trouble."

That evening, with all the important men of the
town assembled in the big front room of the *Herald*
office, Wat Harlow read brokenly the last "reading notice" of Bloomtown's sleeping hero. It was written in
the familiar scrawl that everybody knew, with scarcely
a waver in its lines to tell that a dying hand had
penned it:

"I am going a long journey, but not so far that I
cannot vision your growth. It was the labor of love to
plan for this time. In the gracious wisdom of God it
was not intended that I should enjoy it with you; but
as Moses looked into his promised land, so through the
eyes of the *Herald* I have seen mine. And God, in His
wonderful way, has sent you another optimist to do the
royal work of upbuilding a town.

"My town, my people, I leave to you the greatest
gift I have to offer. I give you my boy, Jap. He is
worthy. Hold up his hands, in memory of
"Ellis Hinton."

As Harlow folded the paper, with hands that trem-
bled, he was not conscious of the fact that hot tears
were streaming down his cheeks. There was an instant

of tense silence. Then Tom Granger walked over to the boy who lay, face downward across the table, arms outspread in abandon of grief. He took one limp hand in his, and a voiceless message went from heart to heart. Jap aroused himself. One by one the men of Bloomtown filed by. No word was spoken, but each man pledged himself to Ellis Hinton as he took the hand of Ellis's boy in a firm clasp. When the others had gone, Wat Harlow remained.

For a moment he stood silent beside the table. Then with a cry of utter heartbreak, he sank to his knees and permitted the bereaved boy to give vent to his long-repressed agony in a saving flood of tears. When they left the office together, there had been welded a friendship that was stronger than years of any other understanding could have given.

Flossy went back to the cottage, and, like the brave helpmeet of such a man as Ellis Hinton must have been, did not sadden the days with her grief. Sometimes, in the little arbor, with J. W. playing at her feet, she sang softly over her sewing:

> "Beautiful isle of Somewhere,
>   Isle of the true, where we live anew,
> Beautiful isle of Somewhere."

It was her advice that caused the boys to fit up a bedroom and living-room on the second floor of the office. It was her idea that separated Bill from the unsteady air of his home. The Judge, heeding the scriptural injunction implied in the immortal words of Moses, "It is not good that man should be alone," had taken unto himself a fourth wife, and Bill had so many rows with his latest stepmother that there was no opposition to the change. Tom Granger observed that it had been so many matrimonial moons since Bill had a mother that he did not know whether he had any real kinfolks at all. It was certain that he knew little of the real meaning of the word "home." Flossy boarded them, and her cottage was their haven of refuge during many a long evening. It was sad comfort, and yet it was the surest comfort, to have her live over again those last days in the mountains, when Ellis's thoughts bridged space and visualized the rebuilding of Bloomtown.

Perhaps Flossy sensed the fact that these evenings were bone and sinew to Jap's manhood. The boy, never careless, was changing to a man of purpose, such as would be the product of Ellis Hinton's training. The stray, born of the union of purposeless, useless Jacky Herron, and Mary, peevish and fretful, changeable and inconstant, had been born again into the likeness of the man who had been almost a demigod to him.

The town was growing, as Ellis had prophesied, and was creeping in three directions across the prairie. It incorporated and began to settle into regular lines. Spring street showed but few gaps in the line of cot-

tages that ran almost all the way from the rear of
Blanke's drug store to Flossy's home, and another line
of modest cottages looked at them from the other side
of the street. A new and fashionable residence place
was laid out, in the extreme south end of town, as far
from the grime and soot of the railroad as possible;
but the substantial old families still clung to their an-
cestral halls in the vicinity of Court House Square.

One day in early spring Bill burst into the office, his
reporter's pad flapping wildly. His brown eyes danced.

"Big doings!" he shouted. "Pap's going to run for
mayor, and he wants the *Herald* to voice the cry of the
town for his services."

"Who said so?" queried Jap, sticking away at the
last legislative report.

"Nobody but him—as far as I can find out," Bill
returned, grinning knowingly. "It seems that they had
a mess of turnip greens, from cellar sprouts, and they
gave him cramps. He was dozing under paregoric when
the idea hit him. It grew like the turnip sprouts, fast
but pale. He wants us to water the sprouts and give
'em air, so that they'll get color in them."

"How much did he send in for the color?" asked Jap,
climbing down interestedly.

The Associate Editor flashed a two-dollar bill.

"I told Pap that if any opposition sprouted, he'd
have to raise the ante," he remarked. "He squealed
loud enough when I squeezed him for this, but I con-

vinced him that we had about done away with charity practice. Told him the *Herald* was out of the amateur class, and after this election the ante 'd be five bones."

"Well," conceded Jap, "as he is Flossy's brother, we'll have to spread it on thick for the low price of introduction. Look up that woodcut of Sames, the Chautauqua lecturer. If you'll chisel off the beard, we can use it for the Judge. I think that we will kill that story you cribbed from the St. Louis *Republic*, about the President's morning canter with his family physician, and run the Judge along the first column. By the way, Bill, it would be a good idea to trace his career from joyous boyhood to the dignity of the judicial office. What judge was he? Since I have known him, he has never 'worked at the bench.' "

Bill grinned wickedly.

"He was judge of live stock at the county fair!"

"Fallen is Cæsar!" Jap exploded. "What can we say about him?"

"Nothin' for certain, as Kelly Jones says," Bill lamented.

"I never tried fiction," Jap averred, "but for the honor of the first aspirant to the office of Mayor of Bloomtown, and the greater glory of our Associate Editor, I am going to plunge."

And plunge he did. When the town read the eulogium that Jap spread upon the front page of the *Herald* it gasped as from a sudden cold plunge, sat up, rubbed its eyes, and concluded that it had somehow failed to understand or appreciate its foremost son. Hollins, the leading grocer, and Bolton, the furniture dealer, had felt the itch for office; and Marquis, the attorney, had stood in his doorway for a week awaiting the delegation that would press upon him the nomination; but all these aspirants faded like poppies in the wake of the reaper. Nobody could be found to buck a sure thing, such as Judge Bowers, backed by the power of the press.

The week after election, the *Herald* sported fifty small flags through its columns, and quoted Wat Harlow's speech in which he declared that Judge William Hiram Bowers was "the noblest Roman of them all." For which Bill accounted to Jap by the astute observation that Rome was a long way off. The Judge hardly caught Wat's meaning, and came into the office to protest.

"I am afeard that folks 'll think we have Catholic blood in the family," he complained, shaking the paper nervously.

"Mystery is the blood of progress, Pap," assured Bill gravely. "If you will notice, the men that get there always have a skeleton rattling a limb now and then."

"Mis' Bowers don't like it," he objected. "I had to quit the Methodists and be immersed in the Baptists afore she'd have me, and now she's fairly tearin' up the wind over this talk about me bein' a Roman. You gotta correct it!"

"We have given you a hundred dollars' worth of advertising for a measly two-dollar bill," declared Jap emphatically. "The columns of the *Herald* are free to news. Advertising at our regular rates. Bill will give you particulars."

"Dollar an inch for display," crisped Bill; "ten cents a line for readers." He seated himself, pencil in hand, as he added, *"payable in advance."*

"Make a flat rate of ten dollars, as it is the Judge," advised Jap judicially.

The Mayor-elect decided to let it alone; but Jap mentioned the fact, in the next issue of the *Herald,* that Judge Bowers had alleged that he was born in New England, of Puritan stock, and had no Italian sympathies—which lucid statement abundantly satisfied Judge and Mrs. Bowers, but set the town to wondering what the Judge was hiding in the dim annals of his past.

CHAPTER XI

"I worked a bunch of passes out of the agent for that Indian medicine show," announced Bill, washing his hands. "Want to take her, Jap?" and he jerked his head in the direction of the front door, where Isabel Granger was passing.

"No; I'm going out to Flossy's a while. I want to talk some things over with her."

There was no further discussion, for at that moment Rosy Raymond floated by, and Bill started out in eager pursuit. Ever since the election, Jap had been obsessed by a disquieting foreboding. One of Mayor Bowers's first official acts was to authorize the opening of a second saloon on Main street, and he was rapidly pushing the work of erecting two new business houses which, rumor declared, were to house other thirst palaces. Hitherto the natives and the surrounding territory had been amply supplied by Holmes; but Bloomtown was growing beyond the reach of one saloon.

Holmes had come across with a double-sized license, under promise of the Mayor that he should continue to have a monopoly of the trade. And when the good people of the various churches waited upon Judge Bow-

ers to protest against what they were disposed to call
the "introduction of Satan into their town," he called
their attention to the need for municipal revenue. If
one saloon was a help, two saloons would double that
help. The town had already begun to show signs of
genuine progress. It had to build a calaboose to take
care of the saloon's patrons, and the regular fines for
plain drunks almost paid the cost of the court that
collected them.

Once Jap thought he detected a sinister reason for
Bill's flushed cheeks and unsteady gait as he passed
hastily through the office on his way to the sleeping
room above. The next morning Bill declared that he
had been a fool, and had paid for his folly with a severe
headache, and Jap, with the delicacy that was Jap's,
let the subject drop. It was becoming fashionable for
the young fellows of the town to assume a tough swag-
ger. Those who had formerly resorted to barn lofts
and musty cellars paraded their sophistication on Main
street, and Bill would rather be dead than out of style.
Jap wanted to talk it over with Flossy, but he had
never found the key to open such poignant confidence.
What right had he to burden Flossy with fresh anxiety? In his loneliness, he yearned for Ellis as he had
never yearned before.

He was sitting on the little front porch, tossing J.
W. on the tough old trotting horse afforded by his two
ill-padded knees, and vaguely wondering how he could

introduce the subject of Bloomtown's swift decay, without wounding Judge Bowers's sister and Bill's aunt, when they heard a great tumult in the vicinity of the medicine show. After a while Bill came up the walk with Rosy.

"What was the racket about?" Jap asked incuriously.

Rosy giggled.

"They wanted to nominate the ugliest man in town, and there was a fight," she said.

"Shut up!" growled Bill. "Haven't you got any sense?"

"Sam Waldron nominated Jap," she sputtered, between giggles.

A hot flush swept over Jap. Always keenly sensitive, he had never armored himself against the playful brutalities of his friends. The shame of being made a subject of ridicule cut deeply.

"Rosy is a fool!" snapped Bill.

"What was the fuss about?" asked Flossy, prompted by a conviction that further revelation would be good for Jap.

"Why, Isabel Granger slapped his face, and Bill jumped in and punched him in the ribs, and the crowd wanted to take him down to the pond and duck him."

Flossy's hand sought Jap's, and she laughed softly.

"That was worth while, boy. How Ellis would have written it up!"

Jap smiled, but the sting was still there. When it was evident that Bill and Rosy expected to spend the evening, he arose with a tired, "Well, I'll be going," and walked around the cottage to the alley gate. He was afraid of meeting some one on Spring street, and he made excuse to his own consciousness that the alley had always been the rational highway between the cottage and the office. He put his hand in his pocket for his key, as he emerged on Main street.

As he approached the door, he saw that some one was sitting on the steps. She sprang up and laid trembling hands on his arm.

"Oh, Jap, you won't mind! You won't let it hurt you? Everybody knows that you are the best-looking man in town. At least I—think so!"

Before he could grasp her arm, the girl was gone. That night Jap lay awake long hours, thinking, thinking. With the morning, reason returned. He had assumed responsibility for Flossy and the boy. He must not think again.

And indeed the next few days gave him little time for thought. Wat Harlow slipped into the office late one afternoon. He wore a furtive look and an appearance of guilt. There was about him a suggestion of gum shoes. Something must be amiss.

"I want to see you alone, Jap," he confessed.

Jap led the way to the little private office. Harlow

was pulling nervously at the stubby mustache that hid his short upper lip.

"In trouble, Wat?" asked Jap anxiously.

"No—not exactly. You see, it's this way——" He coughed apologetically. "The wife had a dream, a funny dream, the other night. She's had curious dreams ever since we took that long trip, to New York and all over, last year, and there may be nothing to it, but——" He lit a fresh cigar, and went at it again. "She says that she saw me going into the Capitol at Washington just as if I belonged there. And she got a notion—— Jap, you know how notionate women are. She thinks—well, she thinks that I might be called to run for the House of Representatives."

"Oh, I see," said Jap, illuminated. "It would sound good for the *Herald* to mention that you are in line?"

"Not rough-like, Jap! Just a little tickle in the ribs, to see what they'd say."

"Oh, I'll fix that," declared Jap, laughing. And the *Herald* flung the hat in the ring for "Harlow, the one honest man."

Jap smiled sadly as he read his copy over. He had a habit of wondering what Ellis would have said. He wondered, too, what attitude the editor of the Barton *Standard* would take. The *Standard* had recently changed hands, and since Bloomtown had pulled a saloon, a sunbonnet factory and two business houses out of Barton, a rapid-fire editorial war had been in progress. By some curious dispensation of Providence, Jones of the *Standard* and Herron of the *Herald* had never met. Jap was not hunting trouble, but the same spirit that prompted him to thrash his tormentors, the day of his advent in Ellis Hinton's town, caused him to wield a fire-tipped pen against the *Standard*.

That opposition to Wat's candidacy would develop, before the nomination, was to be expected; but opposition on the part of the Barton *Standard* would be a purely personal matter, the *Standard* having its own party fights to foster. But that was all Jap feared.

It was even worse than he could have imagined, for Jones dug up a bloody ghost to walk at every political meeting. Not only were all Wat Harlow's sins of omission and commission paraded in the *Standard*, but he was proclaimed as the implacable foe of higher education. In vain did his home paper print his record, of beneficent bills introduced, of committee work on behalf of the district schools, and his great speech setting forth the need of a new normal school building. Jones had one trump card left in his hand, and the day before the convention he played it. It was a handbill, yellow with age and ragged around the edges, but still showing a badly spelled, abominably punctuated story in vermilion ink, with a weeping angel at the top and a rooster and two prancing stallions at the bottom. It proved Wat Harlow the undying foe of the State University.

Despite all the *Herald's* valiant work, that nightmare was Harlow's undoing. The nomination went to a rising politician at the opposite side of the congressional district. A great change had come over the sentiment of the state, since the day when the University had been the favorite tool of the political grafters. Every village had its band of rooters for the Alma Mater, and when the nominating convention came to a close it was apparent that Wat Harlow was hardly an "also ran."

Defeat was galling enough; but the *Standard's* expressions of glee were unbearable. Jap's red hair stood on end, "like quills upon the fretful porcupine," as he stood at his case and threw the type into the stick, hot from the wrath in his soul. The paper was printed, as usual, on Thursday; but Friday brought a change in the even tenor of Bloomtown's way. Jones, of the *Standard*, was a passenger on the eastbound train that left Barton a little after noon. His destination was Bloomtown.

"I am looking for a cross-eyed, slit-eared pup by the name of Herron," was the greeting he flung into the *Herald's* sanctum. The door to the composing room was open. Jap looked up wearily.

"Would you mind sitting down and keeping quiet till I finish setting up this address to the bag of wind that edits the Barton *Standard?*" he said impersonally.

Jones, of the *Standard*, sat down and gaped at the long, lank figure on the stool. A moment he went limp and terrified; then he rallied his courage.

"Do you unwind all at once?" he asked, as Jap disentangled his legs from the stool. "I take back what I said about a pup. You're a full-grown dog, all right. I wasn't looking for a brick-top, either. No wonder you have a weakness for vermilion."

"Better come outside of town," Jap interrupted. "I've been intending to go over to Barton to have a look at you, but it's better thus. I have been stealing space from my readers long enough. They pay for more important things than my private opinion of you. I made up my mind to stop the argument by giving you a hell of a licking, and I've only waited because I didn't care to risk my reputation in a neighboring town. Here it will be different. In the midst of my friends, I hope to fix you so that you'll never try to throw filth on any one again."

Jones arose hastily.

"I want no row," he said uneasily. "I just want an understanding."

"You have the right idea," cried Jap. "You are going to get lots of understanding before you leave Bloomtown."

At that moment the town marshal strolled in, wearing his star pinned on his blue flannel shirt.

"I demand protection," Jones shouted. "This man has threatened me."

"What's the row, Jap?" asked the monitor of peace tolerantly.

"This is Mr. Wilfred Jones, of the Barton *Standard*," was all that Jap said. But the effect was electrical. The man of peace was transformed into an engine of vengeance.

"Going to beat him up?" he yelled. "Go to it, and I'm here, if you need help."

Jap took off his coat, deliberately. He unclasped his cuffs and was in the act of unbuttoning his collar, when the local freight whistled for the crossing below town. With a mighty leap the man from Barton cleared the space between his chair and the door. The strolling populace of Main street was scattered like leaves before a sudden gust of wind. There was an abortive cry of "Stop, thief!" and a bewildered pursuit by several tipsy bums who had been loafing in front of Bingham's saloon, but the appearance of the marshal, wearing a broad grin of satisfaction, dispelled apprehension.

"That was Jones, travelin' light," he explained.

The next issue of the *Standard* failed to mention the editorial visit to Bloomtown; but the scurrilous articles ceased and there was quiet again.

"Did Ellis ever have a fight—that kind of a fight— with anybody?" Jap asked Flossy, when Bill had finished his second-hand recital of the show that "he wouldn't have missed for his farm in Texas." In Bill's heart there arose a mighty resentment against Rosy Raymond, who had enticed him from the office just before Jones arrived.

"Ellis did a good deal of fighting before he got me to fight his battles for him," she said, a whimsical smile in her gentle eyes. "You ought to know, Jap. I never would have had Ellis if he hadn't whipped Brother William."

"But that wasn't a matter of personal grudge," Jap argued. It had seemed to him that somehow he had degraded himself when he went down to Jones's ethical level. "I wanted to use my fists because Jones ridiculed me. When Ellis licked the Judge, it wasn't a personal matter. He did it for me."

"And you did this for—for the honor of Bloomtown," cried Bill, with enthusiasm.

CHAPTER XII

"SOMETHING's broke loose," announced Bill, slamming the door violently. "Pap's bought an automobile." Which illuminative remark indicated that Judge Bowers's mind had expanded to let in a fresh vagary.

Jap looked up inquiringly.

"I reckon it's all on account of Billy Wamkiss," Bill explained.

"Billy who? There never was no such animal," and Jap scowled at the stick in his hand. Conditions in Bloomtown were, as Jim Blanke expressed it, all to the bad. While the political fight was at white heat the Mayor had contrived to have his own way. He was going to "make the town" which Ellis Hinton had failed to make. There would be revenue enough to provide metropolitan improvements, and already there was a metropolitan, perhaps even a Monte Carlo-tan, air to the recently awakened village, as every train disgorged its Saturday evening crowd of gamblers from the city where the lid had gone on with ruthless completeness.

Mrs. Granger had arisen from a sick-bed to call together the women of all the churches to make protest at the licensing of another pool-room, with bar and poker attachment, not two blocks from her home, a stroke that had met its counter stroke when the saloon element threatened to boycott Granger's bank and open a rival financial institution in one of the store-rooms of the recently erected hotel that faced the Court House Square, half a block away. Another crowd, the men with store-rooms and cottages to rent, promised to carry all their banking business to Barton, if Granger didn't "sit on his wife good and proper."

"Never was no such animal?" Bill repeated. "Wake up, Jap. Don't you know who Billy Wamkiss is?"

"Never heard of the guy," Jap insisted.

"He's that greasy, wall-eyed temperance lecturer that's been stringing the town for a week."

"Humph!" Jap snorted. "Time for you to wake up, Bill. You brought in the ad yourself, and you wrote the account of the first lecture. The columns of the *Herald* will bear me out that the reverend gentleman's name is Silas Parsons."

"Yes, that's his reverend name," Bill snorted. "When he's the advance agent of a rotgut whiskey house over in Kentucky that supplies fancy packages to all the dry territory around here, he's plain Billy Wamkiss."

"Oh, that's his game!" Jap sat up, his gray eyes wide with astonishment. "How did you get next to it?"

"Your good friend, Wilfred Jones, put me wise. He didn't mean to, but he let it slip out when he wasn't

watching. I ran into him over in Barton this morning
and he was roasting Bloomtown as usual. Said we were
a bunch of Rubes, to fall for a raw proposition like
Billy Wamkiss, dressed up as a temperance lecturer.
And then he went on to say that my daddy would get
richer'n he already is, from his rake-off on the moisture
that'll be injected into the town after she goes dry. He
said he met Wamkiss in Chicago three years ago, and
he's been doing a rattling business all over the country
—deliver lectures on the evils of the Demon Rum that'd
bring tears to the eyes of a potato; dry up the territory, with the help of the churches; and then fill up the
town with drug stores. That's his program, and it's
going to work here, thanks to my amiable and honorable father."

Jap was silent. He had no words with which to ex-
press his emotions. Bill went out on the street, his
reporter's pad under his arm. In half an hour he returned.

"It's worse—I mean more incriminating—than I
thought, Jap," he said, as he drew his partner into the
private office and shut the door.

"Did you attend that meeting at the Baptist
Church?" Jap asked anxiously.

"Yes, and I had to dig out before it was over. I
wanted to explode, and blow up the whole bunch of
idiots and crooks. Pap and Wamkiss, alias Parsons,
have formed some kind of a Templar lodge, and my

daddy's got himself elected secretary. They're going to dry up Bloomtown. Fancy it! They did a lot of crooked work over at the Court House, so as to make it look as if all the licenses would expire at the same time. Holmes is the only one that's likely to squeal, because he's paid his second fee, and the others have only a few months to run. They'll make it up to Holmes, I reckon, rather'n have him give the snap away. Of course, Jap, I haven't got the goods for any of this. I just put two and two together while I was listening to the speeches, especially my father's speech."

"Bill"—Jap laid his hand on Bill's arm—"you made the mistake of your career when you picked that owl for a daddy. He has made more trouble than three towns could stand up against. First, he throws the place wide open and takes all the stray saloons and gambling dens to his bosom; and just when we have a reputation for being the toughest town on the road and doing a land-office business in sin, he is—he is fool enough to try to pull off a stunt like this. What becomes of his plea for municipal revenue when he turns saloons into drug stores?"

"Well, the lid's going on," Bill returned. "The preachers and the ladies are strong for it, and the right honorable Mayor announced that he was the Poo Bah that was going to put up the shutters."

"Better order a granite," Jap muttered, as he returned to the composing room.

And his prediction was well founded, for the town had become so used to its "morning's morning" that it fairly ravened for the blood of Mayor Bowers. The *Herald* office became a forum for indignant orators, while the Mayor strutted proudly up and down Main street, with the black-coated Parsons, feeling that the eyes of the world were glued on him.

"Parsons! Bah!" spluttered Kelly Jones, who had driven four miles with his empty jug. "Ef the town has got any git-up, it'll ride him and that old jackass of a mayor on a rail."

"Judge Bowers is the honored father of our Associate Editor," informed Jap gravely.

As Bill looked up he thumped the galley he was carrying against the case and pied the whole column. After he had said what he thought about the catastrophe, Kelly grinned appreciatively.

"Them's my sentiments, Bill. Ef you love your pappy, you'd better let him go, along of Parsons, 'cause there's goin' to be doin's around Bloomtown that'll hurt his pride. Parsons! They say out our way that his right name's Wamkiss."

The turgid tide of popular sentiment caused Mayor Bowers some uneasiness; but before anything could happen five new drug stores were opened for business and things moved placidly along again. Barton began to refer to "our neighbor, Bumtown," and it was reported that two blind tigers prowled in the environs of the railroad station.

"Bill," said Jap one morning, "this won't do. We'll have to raise hell in this town. This is Ellis's town, and we're not going to let a dod-blinged mugwump like your asinine daddy ruin it. Bill, if you have got any speech to make, get ready. If you can't stand for my program, name your price, for the *Herald* is going to everlastingly lambaste William Bowers, Senior."

"Pull the throttle and run 'er wild," Bill retorted, as he ducked down behind the press and dragged forth a box from the corner. "I'm going to get out that last lot of cuts that Ellis made," he continued. "Kelly Jones knows sense. If I remember right, Ellis had twenty-five cuts of jacks for the stock bill. We will stick every blamed one of 'em in next week's issue, and label 'em Mayor Bowers. He has killed the town with his ideas. What can we do with him but hang him?"

When the *Herald* appeared the following Thursday afternoon, the town quit business to read the war cry of Ellis's boy. It was a flaming sword, hurled at the Board of Aldermen. Bowers, foaming with wrath, stormed into the office.

"You take all that back," he yelled, "or I'll put you out of this here building. I've told you times enough this office belongs to me. I never turned it over to Ellis."

Jap stuck type, deadly calm on the surface of his

being. Bill shifted uneasily, his hands clinched, his
ruddy face glowing.

"You hear me?" bawled the irate Mayor.

Jap turned to consult his copy. Before the act
could be imagined Bowers had struck him over the head
with the revolver he dragged from his pocket. Jap fell,
crumpling to the floor, the blood spurting across the
type. For an instant there was horrified silence. Then,
with a howl like that of a wild beast, Bill threw himself
upon his father. But for the intervention of Tom
Granger, who had followed the Mayor because he
scented trouble, there would have been a quick finish
to the pompous career of Bill Bowers's progenitor, for
Bill had wrested the pistol from his father's hand and
was pressing it against the temple of the worst scared
coward Bloomtown had ever seen. There was a sharp
tussle between the broad-shouldered banker and the
frenzied youth. Several men rushed in from the street.

"Let me go!" shouted Bill, "for if he's killed Jap he's
got to die."

They were carrying Jap out of the composing room,
limp and bleeding.

"Let him alone, Bill," Tom counselled wisely. "Let
your father alone, for if Jap is dead, we'll lynch him."

Jap was pretty weak when they brought the Mayor's
resignation up from the calaboose for him to read. A
representative delegation stood around his bed.

"Let the Judge out, for Bill's sake," Jap said.

"We'd better keep him locked up for his own sake," declared Tom Granger. "For in Bill's present frame of mind he's likely to make an orphan of himself."

Flossy came in from the little sitting-room and leaned over the bed.

"I am going to see Brother William," she said quietly. "I am going to take Brent Roberts with me. William will give you boys a quitclaim bill to this property, for this dastardly deed."

She was an impersonation of righteous wrath as she swept into the jail, followed by Bloomtown's leading attorney. Judge Bowers had said more than once that Flossy had a willing tongue, but its full willingness was never conceived until she descended upon him that eventful day.

An arrangement, made by Ellis just before his departure, gave the contents of the office to the boys, on regular payments to Flossy. The ground on which the new building stood had been deeded to Ellis and Flossy on their wedding day; but the building, presumed to be a gift to Ellis, had been reclaimed by Bowers; it was held, however, as Bill's share in the firm. As yet no occasion had arisen that demanded the settling of the question of ownership. Whenever the Judge had an attack of bile he came into the office to remind Bill and Jap that the building was still his.

For one heated hour Flossy detailed the past, present and future of her cowering brother. When she left him he was a wiser, and probably a sadder, man, for she had deprived him of his weapon.

There was a big bonfire on the circus grounds, and a celebration in Court House Square that night. The next day there was a great vacuum in the City Hall, for the Board of Aldermen resigned unanimously. A special election was called, and before Jap was strong enough to sit at his case he had been elected Mayor of Bloomtown.

He looked sadly from the window of his bedroom, after the joyous crowd of serenaders that had come to congratulate him. Bill had followed in their wake, to escort Rosy home. It was late. The clock in the Presbyterian church spire chimed twelve, as he stood alone. He took his hat from the rack and went cautiously downstairs. On the pavement he paused a moment to steady himself. His head still reeled after any unwonted exertion. Then he walked slowly up Main street, across the railroad tracks, and out to the quiet village whose inhabitants slept 'neath marble and sod. Standing beside the grave of his first friend, he said:

"Ellis, make the town proud of your boy. Help me to be your right hand. If I can only fulfill your plan, I am willing that no other ambition be fulfilled."

A lonely night bird called softly. The willow branches waved in the breeze. Thick darkness hung over the City of the Dead. Suddenly the moon peered through the clouds, flooding the night with beauty, and Jap read from the stone the last message of Ellis:

"I go, but not as one unsatisfied. In God's plan, my work will live."

CHAPTER XIII

"Now that you've got it, Jap," asked Tom Granger, "what are you going to do with it?" Jap looked silently from the door.

"He put in about eight hours of thinking about that himself," Bill averred. "News is that ten saloons are loaded on freight cars, waiting word from Jap."

"You'll have to strike a happy medium," suggested Tom. "I know that you are the boy to deliver the goods."

"Ellis wasn't against saloons," commented Bill, "so Jap won't have that to chew over. Ellis wasn't either for or against 'em."

"No," Tom said seriously, "Ellis was dead set against hypocrisy. He hated a liar and a grafter worse than a murderer. He knew that the way to make people want a thing was to tell 'em they couldn't have it."

Jap's face was grave. A panorama of wretched pictures moved slowly before his wandering gaze, pictures that began and ended in Mike's place, in the half-forgotten village of Happy Hollow. He aroused himself with a start.

"I'm going to put it up to the new Board to allow

as many saloons as want to, to come in," he said shortly.

Tom Granger let go a shrill whistle.

"At the license asked," continued Jap calmly. "The license will be three thousand dollars a year, and strict enforcement of all laws. At the first break, the lid will fall."

"Jumping cats!" howled Tom. "Where will you get the saloon that'll pay that?"

Jap smiled wearily. "I am not hunting a saloon for Bloomtown," he said, and turned toward the door in time to bump into Isabel Granger, her arms full of bundles. She blushed and dimpled prettily.

"I am looking for my papa," she cried, pinching Tom's cheek with her one free hand. "I want you to carry these packages for me."

"Run along, pet. I'm busy."

"You look it," she reproved. "I simply can't carry all these things. My arm is almost broken now, and the dressmaker has to have them."

"Jap will tote them for you," chuckled Tom, watching the blood rush over Jap's sensitive face. To his surprise, Jap took the bundles and walked out with Isabel. He looked after them approvingly.

"Now there goes the likeliest boy in the state," he declared. "It's plumb funny the way he's got of getting right next to your marrow bones. I wish I had a boy like him."

"No great matter," drawled Bill, with tantalizing indefiniteness.

Tom looked up at him quizzically, as he picked absently at the pile of exchanges. Something in the young man's tone piqued him.

"If Jap wasn't so all-fired conscientious," Bill blurted, "you'd have a son, in quick order."

"Lord!" exploded Tom. "Dunderhead that I am!" He slapped his thigh, and a great, joyous laugh set his shoulders to heaving. "Bill, you're a genius for spying out mysteries. How did you get on to it?"

"Mysteries!" shouted Bill. "Why, everybody in Bloomtown, including Isabel, knows that Jap is fairly sapheaded about her."

"Well, what's hampering him?" inquired Tom. "Why don't he confide in me?"

"Confide your hat!" remarked Bill crisply. "Isabel will die of old age before Jap asks her. You see, he is such a durn fool that he thinks he isn't good enough for her. When the Lord made Jap Herron He made a man, I tell you!"

"Who said He didn't?" stormed Tom. "I can't know what is in the boy's mind, can I? What do you want me to do, kidnap him and get his consent? Bill, you're a fool. You needn't tell me that Jap Herron is such a mealy-mouth."

"All I know is that he won't ask Isabel," Bill said gloomily. "I'd like to get married myself, but as long

as Jap stays single, I stick too." And thinking of
Rosy's blue eyes, he sighed heavily.

"It beats me, the way young folks do. It was different when I went courting," Tom muttered, turning
to go.

At the door he met Kelly Jones, who had come in to
inquire what Jap intended to do about the "licker"
business. He was too busy with his fall plowing to be
running over to Barton for his jug of good cheer, and
he didn't like the brand he could get at Bingham's
drug store, on Doc Connor's prescription. While he
was still holding forth, Jap came in, with half-a-dozen
constituents, all busy with the same problem. Bill took
up his notebook and wandered out. At Blanke's drug
store he met Isabel. She motioned for him to come back
in the store.

"What do you want to know, Iz?" he asked with the
familiarity born of long years of propinquity. "Reckon you want to ask what everybody else wants to know
—when is Jap going to get a saloon?"

"You are too smart, Bill Bowers," she retorted, with
annoyance. She had had a subject of more personal
nature on the tip of her tongue. "I think that Jap
will be able to answer his own questions without any
help from you."

"It is to be hoped that he will make a better stagger
at answering than he does at asking," remarked Bill
shortly.

"Now, Bill Bowers, *just* what do you mean?" she demanded, her black eyes flashing angrily.

"What's the use?" said Bill, in disgust. "Rosy says that she's going to Kansas this fall, and I just will have to let her go because I can't ask her to stay."

"Pity about you," she snapped. "Thought you said Jap couldn't ask."

"I did," assented Bill, "for if he had gumption enough to get married, or even go courting, I might get by. But as long as he sticks alone I'm going to stick, too."

Isabel's face flamed. She stooped to pick up a bit of paper.

"What do you want to tell me about it for?" she complained. "My goodness, I'm not to blame."

"You are," stormed Bill. "Jap knows that he is not your equal, and he never will marry."

"Who said that Jap Herron was not more than the equal of any man on earth?" she blazed. "If Jap will ask me, I'll marry him to-morrow."

She whirled away in her wrath, and ran into the arms of Jap Herron, standing half paralyzed with the wonder of it. Bill, who had been watching the unconscious Jap approaching for several minutes, discreetly withdrew.

"Gee!" he said, "but they ought not to be kissing in such a public place."

There were a dozen customers in the store, but

neither Jap nor Isabel knew it. And it is to the credit of Bloomtown that they all looked the other way, as they hurriedly transacted their business and departed. Blanke declared afterward that he filled fifteen prescriptions with epsom salts in his abstraction, and accidentally cured Doc Horton's best paying patient. Moss, the paper hanger, went out with his rolls of paper, and hung the border on the walls, instead of the siding. The mistakes reported were legion; but the town was all courting Isabel with Jap, at heart.

Bill rambled into the bank and suggested that Tom go over to Blanke's and lead Jap and Isabel out, as Blanke might want to close the store. Half an hour later Tom came from the drug store, with an arm locked with each of the glowing pair. Straight across Main street they marched, and down the shady walk that flanked the little park until they were opposite the front gate of the Granger home. Then they went in to break the news to Isabel's invalid mother.

Flossy heard about it, almost before Jap had awakened to his own joy, and he never knew of the hour she spent in passionate grief. In some vague way it seemed to tear open the old wound. Without knowing why, she resented the fact that Isabel's brunette beauty had won Jap. She told herself that it was not a fitting match for him. Flossy, in her maternal soul, had looked to heights undreamed of by the retiring boy. She had planned a future for him that would be sadly hampered by marriage with a village belle. But only smiles met him when he brought Isabel to her, his plain features glorified by joy in her possession.

Somehow the story of Jap Herron, the youthful Mayor of Bloomtown, his advent in its environs, and the story of his romance with the banker's daughter, crept into the country press, was carried over into the city papers and flung broadcast, so that friend and foe might seek him out. One dreary fall day, when the rain was beating sullenly down on the sodden leaves, a haggard, dirty woman straggled into the office.

"I'm lookin' for Jasper Herron," she mumbled. "They told me I'd find him in here."

Jap looked at her in horror. His heart sank.

"I am his poor old mother, that he run away from and left to starve," she said viciously.

And Jap, just on the threshold of his greatest happiness, was turned aside by this grizzly, drunken phantom from the past.

CHAPTER XIV

Little J. W. crawled out from under Bill's case, his brown eyes wide with surprise at this vagrant who called Jap "son."

"Run like sin," counselled Bill, in a whisper, "and bring your mother. She will know what to do."

While the boy went to do his bidding, Bill slipped out of the rear door of the office and was waiting in front of the bank when Flossy came hurrying along.

"Oh, Bill, what has Jap said?" she asked breathlessly. From J. W.'s lisping description—he always lisped when he was excited—she had come to fear the worst.

"Nothing," said Bill bluntly. "He's sitting at his case, sticking type as if he was hired by the minute."

"And she—that awful woman?"

"Gee!" Bill spat the word. "You don't know anything yet. Wait till you lamp her over."

"That bad, Bill?"

"Worse," muttered Bill. And when Flossy came inside and looked into the little inner office where the woman sprawled, half asleep and muttering incoherently, the fumes of liquor and the presence of filth all

145

too evident, her stomach rebelled and she retreated swiftly. Softly she slipped into the composing room through the wide-open door. Timidly she approached Jap and touched his arm. He looked at her with eyes utterly hopeless.

"Oh, Jap, what can I do?"

"You cannot do anything," his voice flat and emotionless. "No one can. Could you take her in? No! She is impossible, and yet—she is my mother. Perhaps if I had stayed with her it would have been different, so I must make up for it."

Flossy looked into his set face in affright.

"I am going away—with her." Jap's tones were calm. "You can see, Flossy, that it is the only way. I cannot be Mayor of Ellis's town with such a disgrace to shame me. I must give up Isabel and—and the *Herald.*"

Flossy clung to his arm.

"Listen to me, Jap Herron," she cried shrilly. "You shall not do it! You shall not let this horrible old woman drag you down in the dirt."

Jap smiled sadly.

"What could I do, Flossy? She must be cared for. She has been all over town. Everybody has seen her. They know the truth, that my mother is—what she is."

Suddenly he threw himself forward on the case and began to sob, such hard, racking sobs as might tear his very breast. Flossy threw her arms around him and cried aloud. Bill stood in the little private office, looking down upon the snoring woman with a murderous glare. He turned as Tom Granger came noiselessly from the outer office and stood beside him. Grief was in Granger's face.

"I heard what Jap said just now," he whispered, "and he is right. It would be impossible for him to stay with her in the town. She has ruined Jap."

"You're a gol-dinged fool," shouted Bill, dragging him across the big office and out of the front door. "Pretty sort of friend you are, anyway. I'll fight you, or a half-dozen like you, if you murmur a word like that to Jap."

He whirled as his father ambled up the street, his round face wearing a grin.

"What is that greasy smirk for?" demanded Bill. "If you have any business in the *Herald* office, spit it out."

"I knowed it would come out sooner or later," spluttered Bowers, shifting his position to avoid a pool in the pavement, left by the recent rain. "With half an eye, anybody could see the mongrel streak in——"

He stopped as his son advanced swiftly toward him.

"What kind of a streak?" he threatened. "I dare you to say that again, and hitch anybody's name to it."

"Why, William," expostulated his father, "you shorely ain't goin' to have Jap and his mammy hitched up to the *Herald?* Barton 'll ride Bloomtown proper."

"It will give Jones a whack at the *Herald*," suggested Granger mildly.

"And it will be his last whack!" foamed Bill. "For I'll finish him and his filthy paper before I go to the pen for burning down the *Herald* office. The day that Jap Herron leaves the *Herald*, there will be the hell-firedest bonfire that Bloomtown ever saw!" His eyes were blazing. "Get away from here," he cried fiercely, "you—you milksop friends!"

He stopped as Isabel, her eyes swollen from crying, crossed the street. She had come across the corner of the park, and her face was white and drawn. Bill stepped up into the doorway and awaited her.

"I want to speak to Jap," she said, as he barred the passage.

"What do you want with him?" Bill demanded truculently. "Because he is packing all the load now that he can stand, and you ain't going to add another chip to it. Give me your old engagement ring, and I'll pitch it in the hell-box. I reckon that's what you came for."

She pushed him aside, her eyes blazing with wrath.

"Get out of my way, Bill Bowers. You never did have any sense. Let me by!"

She flung herself past him and ran into the composing room. At sight of Flossy, she paused. Flossy raised her head from Jap's shoulder and looked defiantly at the girl, but only for a second. She knew, in that glance. Softly she crept out as Isabel, with a heart-shaking cry, ran to Jap and threw herself against him.

"Take me in your arms, Jap," she cried stormily, "for I love you."

Jap stared up, dully, for an instant. Then, forgetting all but love, he opened his arms and clasped her to his heart. Bill rushed outside after Flossy.

"I never knew that she was the real goods," he said remorsefully, wiping his eyes.

"Get a wagon from the grocer," Flossy said, decisive again. "I am going to take her home with me."

"Meaning that?" Bill flipped his thumb toward Jap's mother.

"Send her up to the house, and I will have a doctor, and some one to bathe her and clean her up. Maybe after she is clean and sober, she won't be so dreadful."

When Jap came out of his stupor enough to try to put Isabel away, he discovered what Flossy had done. With Isabel clinging to him, he walked with downcast head through the streets that lay between the *Herald* office and Flossy's cottage.

His mother was in bed, clean and yet disgusting in her drunken sleep. He forgot Isabel, silent by his side, as he stood looking down upon the blotched and sunken face, thinking what thoughts God only knew. He seemed years older as he walked out again, after the doctor had told him that nothing could be determined until she had slept the liquor off. Slowly and silently he and Isabel walked past the row of neat cottages until they reached Main street. On the corner Jap paused.

"You must go home, Isabel," he said brokenly. "Sweetheart, I understand, and I know that you are the bravest girl in the world. But you must leave me now."

"I will not," she declared. "I want you to take me right down to the office and send for a license. I am going to marry you, and show this town what I think of you!"

"But I cannot let you," Jap said simply. "I know—you don't."

"Then," said Isabel defiantly, "I will go back to Flossy's and take care of your mother until you are ready to talk sense."

Jap looked at her helplessly. They were in front of Blanke's drug store. Jim Blanke stepped outside and grasped Jap's hand. Isabel looked proudly up at him, her arm drawn tightly through Jap's. As they passed down the street, citizens sprang up, apparently from nowhere, and clasped Jap's hand in a fraternal grip. Isabel peered into his silent face. The tears were streaming unheeded down his cheeks. Her father frowned as they appeared at the door of the bank.

"Papa," she called resolutely, "you coming with us?"

He stood gnawing at his lips, his face overcast. An

instant he battled with his pride and his love for the boy. Then, with his old heartiness, he clapped Jap on the shoulder.

"Straighten your shoulders, lad. We're all your friends!" And the storm cloud lightened.

All that night Jap paced the floor of the office, while Bill, too sympathetic for sleep, tossed in the room above and swore at fate. It was noon the next day when little J. W. came in to say that Mrs. Herron was awake and wanted to see her son.

She was half sitting among the pillows when Jap entered. Flossy had drawn the muslin curtains, to soften the garish light as it fell on her seamed and shame-scarred face. She peered up at him from blood-shot, sunken eyes.

"You look like your pappy's folks, Jasper," she croaked. "And they tell me you air a fine, likely boy, and follerin' in the trade of your gran'pap. I wisht that I had a known where you was, long ago. I have had a hard life, Jasper. Your step-pa beat me, and that's more'n your pappy ever done. He died of the trimmins, three year ago, and I have been wanderin' every since, huntin' my childurn. But Aggie's a big-bug now, and she drove me off. And Fanny's goin' to a fine music school, and sent me word that she'd have me put in a sanitary if I bothered her. She saw a piece about you in the paper, and sent it to me. So I tramped thirty mile to come."

Her face was pathetic in its misery. She sank back in the pillows and closed her eyes. Jap leaned down and drew the covers tenderly over her arms. She opened her eyes, at the touch, and looked up at him sadly.

"Thanky, Jasper," she mumbled. "You be-ant mad?"

He patted her cheek softly, and the sunken eyes lighted with a smile of weary contentment. Then the lids fluttered, like the last effort of a spent candle, and she slept. Like one in the maze of a vague, uncertain dream, Jap went back to the office. Unconsciously he took the familiar way, through the alley. Automatically he climbed to his stool and began setting up the editorial that had been interrupted by his mother's coming the previous day.

At sunset Bill touched his shoulder softly. Jap raised his head from his hands.

"Your—your mother never woke up after you left her, Jap," he said huskily.

CHAPTER XV

B ILL looked up as a long, lank form glided surreptitiously into the office.

"Been a long time since *you* drifted our way," he commented, as the form resolved itself into the six-foot length of Kelly Jones.

"Might' nigh three month," averred Kelly grimly. "I've been tradin' over at Barton. Couldn't stand for Jap's damfoolishness. Had to buy my licker there, and just traded there. It's twelve mile from my farm to Barton, and four mile to Bloomtown. Spring's comin' on, and work to do. I hate to take that trip every time the wife needs a spool o' thread. Did you get my letter, sayin' to stop the paper?"

"Stopped it, didn't we?" queried Bill crisply, scattering the type from the financial report of Bloomtown into the case.

"Yes," assented Kelly, "you did. What'd you do it for?"

"Not forcing the *Herald* on anybody," announced Bill glibly. "Got past that. We used to hold 'em up and feed the *Herald* to them, but we don't have to do it now."

"I hear tell that Jap made Tim Simpson night marshal. Why, he run a blind tiger beyond the water tank," exclaimed Kelly. "I reckon Jap didn't know that."

"Just because he did know it, he made Tim night marshal," declared Bill, flinging the last type into the box and descending from the stool. "Just you stroll down the tracks in either direction, and see if you can find a whisker or a tawny hair from the tip of any tiger's tail lying loose along the way. Jap knows several things, Kelly, my boy, and he is fighting fire with fire. Tim Simpson understands the operations of the kind of menagerie that usually flourishes in a dry town, and Jap put him on his honor. He's so conscientious that he goes over to Barton to get full. He won't drink it here. He's got pride in making Bloomtown the whitest town in the state. But explain the return of the prodigal. How come your feet in our dust again?"

"Well," said Kelly shamefacedly, "the wife said that I was a durn fool. I stopped the *Herald* and subscribed for the *Standard*—and a pretty standard it is! While Jap Herron was cleanin' up, it was slingin' muck at him. The wife read it, and one day she goes up to Barton and starts an argument with Jones. I reckon she had the last word. If she didn't, it was the fu'st time. She come home so rip-snortin' mad that she threatened to lick me if I didn't tackle Jones. Well, to keep peace in the family, I run in to see him the next time I went to Barton. Well, Jones put it up to me, if Jap was doin' much for Bloomtown in havin' unlicensed drug stores, instid of regular saloons."

"Sure sign that you don't know the news," said Bill, unfolding a copy of the *Herald*. "Since last Saturday night there has been only one drug store in Bloomtown. That's Blanke's, and Jim Blanke wouldn't sell liquor on anybody's prescription but Doc Hall's, and Doc Hall would let you die of snake-bite, if nothing but whiskey would cure you. Any other drug stores that may open up in this town 'll have to pattern after Blanke's or out they go."

Kelly took the paper up and scanned its columns. He snorted.

"Well, I do declare! I see that might' nigh all the doctors have packed up and are threatenin' to leave town. Well, there wa'n't enough doctorin' to keep twenty of 'em in cash nohow."

"You ought to have heard Jap's speech when they were putting a plea for local option," said Bill. "My pap has carried a sore ear against Jap's reign ever since he was elected to fill out that unexpired term, and he stirred up a lot of bellyaches among the guzzlers. It was a sickening mess, because the whole town knows that my daddy can't stand even the smell of liquor. It wouldn't be so bad—so hypocritical, if he really liked it and was used to it. As I was telling you, he and the old booze gang had been burning the midnight dip to plan a crimp for Mayor Herron, when that local option idea struck him. Well, Jap got up and made a speech, calling their attention to the bonds we voted, and the sound financial condition back of those bonds; the granitoid pavement on Main street, the electric light plant that's going up, and the water works, and sewers that are under way—all managed since the town went dry. Then he nominated Tom Granger for mayor, and what do you reckon they did?"

"Seein' as how he ain't mayor," said Kelly, with a twinkle, "I allow they done nothin'."

"Why," said Bill, his brown eyes kindling, "they arose as one man and yelled, 'We want Jap Herron!' and that settled it."

The farmer stood in the middle of the office, his arms gesticulating and his head bobbing with animation, as Jap hurried in. He gazed at the back of Kelly's familiar slicker incredulously.

"What!" he hailed joyously, "our old friend of the sorghum barrel! Where have you been hibernating? Surely a cure for sore eyes," and Jap seized his shoulder and whirled him around so that he could grasp his hand.

"Chipmunking in Barton," prompted Bill. "This sadly misguided farmer has been lost but now is found."

"The Missus sent a package to Mis' Flossy. You and Bill 'll eat it, I reckon," and he produced a parcel from his pocket. "She said if Ellis was here, he'd appreciate it. It's sausage that she made herself. And —and she sent a dollar for the paper. She wants the *Herald*."

"And what about Kelly?" Jap asked, a wave of memory sweeping over him.

"Just you write it down that Kelly Jones is a yaller pup," said Kelly morosely.

"Never!" declared Jap heartily. "Misled, perhaps, but with a heart of gold."

Kelly groped for his handkerchief.

"I've got on the water wagon, Jap," he sniffled. "I reckon I kin get along without the stuff. Sary hid my jug, and I done 'thout it for a week, and I felt fine. I am goin' to make a stagger at it, if I do fall down."

Jap pushed him into a chair.

"Why, you old rascal," he cried, "you have backbone enough to do anything you will to do. Move into town and help us turn the wheels."

Kelly wiped his nose on the tail of his slicker as he started for the door.

"Don't happen to need any 'lasses, do you?" he grinned.

Jap flung an empty ink bottle after him. When quiet had returned to the office, he said, as he hung his hat on the nail:

"Isabel wants to learn to stick type."

"Funny," said Bill shortly, "so does Rosy, and they

hate each other like Pap hates beer. Pretty mix-up we'll have on our hands."

"That's all nonsense, Bill. Rosy can't help liking Isabel."

Bill scanned the copy on his hook, his eyes narrowing.

"Appears like she can," he muttered.

"Now, Bill, this won't do," argued Jap earnestly. "We can't afford to have dissension in such a vital matter. You must talk to Rosy."

"You can have the job," waived Bill, picking up a type. "Isabel said that Rosy was shallow and only skin-deep, and Rosy heard about it. Isabel Granger is not so much——"

He stopped abruptly as Jap's hand went up in pained alarm.

"Look here, Bill, are we going to let the chatter of women come between us? There is something deeper holding us together than the friendship of a day. Give me your hand, Bill, and tell me that it is Ellis's work and not these trifles that you care for. We have a work to do, you and I."

Bill threw the stick upon the case and grasped Jap's outstretched hand. Tears glistened in his eyes.

"Better than all the loves in the world, I love you, Jap," he stormed. Jerking his hat from the nail, he strode out to walk off the emotionalism he decried.

That afternoon he strove manfully to show Isabel

how to put type in the stick upside down, and to save her feelings he stealthily corrected her faulty work, suppressing a grin at Jap's pride in her first attempt. Bill shook his head sadly as they strolled out together, Jap's eyes drinking in the girl's slender beauty.

"Petticoat government 'll get old Jap tripped up," he complained to the office cat. "And then where'll I be? When Jap marries I'll play second fiddle. Come seven, come 'leven!" and he snapped his fingers in the air.

CHAPTER XVI

THE sun was streaming through the east windows. Jap looked anxiously up and down the street. Bill had not been home all night. This was a state of affairs alarming to Jap. He walked back to the table and turned the exchanges over restlessly.

"I wonder if the boy could have persuaded that butterfly to elope with him, as he threatened he would, when her mother cut up so rough," he worried.

Tim Simpson came in and peered around furtively.

"Bill is drunk as a lord," he announced in a stage whisper. "I've got him in the back room of the calaboose, to sober up without the news leakin'."

Jap paled.

"Bill drunk?" he faltered. "Who got him into it? Is he asleep, Tim?"

"Lord, no! If he was, I would 'a' left him out when he come to, and said no word to you about it. But I'm plum scared about him. He's chargin' up and down like a Barnum lion. I reckon as how you'd better mosey down there and try to ca'm him."

As Jap walked rapidly down the alley beside the night marshal, he asked:

"Did you try to talk to him?"

"Yes," said Simpson ruefully. "He kicked me out and was chasin' after me when I slammed the door on him. He's blind crazy loaded. I fu'st seen him after number nine pulled in, so I think he come on her. He was mutterin' and shakin' his fist when he hove in sight. I got him and steered him into the jug without much trouble, and it was only a hour ago that he started this ragin' and ravin'."

As they entered the jail, sounds of tramping feet and mutterings reached their ears. Bill's swollen, blotched face and reddened eyes appeared behind the grating.

"Let me out of here!" he shouted. "You'll get a broken head for this, you old mule." He shook the grating furiously.

"Bill," said Jap slowly, "do you want to come with me, or do you want me to stay here with you till you've had a bath and a good sleep?"

Bill laughed discordantly.

"A sleep! A sleep!" he cried. "Yes, a long, long sleep. As soon as you take me out of this hell-hole, I'll take a sleep that'll last."

Jap opened the door and stepped inside.

"Don't come any nearer," warned Bill. "I'm too filthy, Jap. But let me stay as I am till it's over."

He sat down on the cot and stared crazily into the

corridor. Jap sat down beside him and drew his arm around his shoulder, with the tenderness of a woman.

"Tell me about it, Bill, boy," he counselled gently. "Tim, you may leave us."

Bill sat a long time, staring sullenly at the floor.

"Well, this is a hell of a display for me to bring to Bloomtown," he declared at last. "I should have ended it in Jones's town. If I hadn't been so dumb with rotgut that I didn't know what I was doing, I would be furnishing some excitement for the Bartonites this morning. The finest place in the world to die in—it isn't fit to live in."

Jap shook him briskly.

"Straighten up, Bill, and tell me what kind of a mess you have been in."

Bill laughed wildly. After a moment he dragged a letter from his pocket. Jap read:

"When you read this, I will be the wife of Wilfred Jones, the Editor of the Barton *Standard*. Maybe you will be pleased? I prefer to marry a real editor, not the half of Jap Herron."

The letter was signed, "Rosalie," but the affectation carried none of the elements of a disguise. To Jap it was the crowning insult. Crushing the silly note in his hand, he threw it from him. Standing up, he drew Bill to his feet.

"We are going home," he said curtly. "When you

are sober I will tell you how disappointed I am in my brother."

The news that Bill had been jilted spread over Bloomtown like fire in a stubble-field, and deep resentment greeted the announcement that Jones of the *Standard* had scored another notch against the *Herald*.

Bill, sullen and defiant, had battled it out in the room above the office. All the vagaries of a sick mind were his. Murder, suicide, mysterious disappearance, chased each other across the field of his vision, and ever the specter of suicide returned to grin at him. For a day and a night Jap sat beside his bed, talking, soothing, comforting. Finally he made this compact:

"To show you that I love you better than myself, Bill, I am going to promise that I will not marry until you are cured of this blow. Not a word, Bill! Happiness would turn to ashes if I accepted it at your cost. How far I am to blame in your trouble, I can only guess. I am not going to preach philosophy. I am only going to plead my love for you."

He took the revolver from the drawer and laid it on the table beside Bill.

"If you are the boy I think you are, you will be sticking type when I come back from Flossy's. If you are a coward, I will not grieve to find you have taken the soul that God gave you and flung it at His feet."

Not trusting himself to look back, he hurried down

the stairs. His heart was heavy with dread as he locked
the office and walked blindly to the cottage where all
his problems had been carried. He could not talk to
Flossy, but, sitting beside her on the little front porch,
he fought the mad impulse to run back to the office.
He strained his ears for the sound that he was praying
not to hear.

Two hours he sat there, fighting with his fears, the
longest hours of his life. Flossy sat as silent. No one
knew Jap as Flossy did. Smoothing his tumbled hair
and stroking his tightly clenched hands were her only
expressions. Futile indeed would words be now. The
tragedy that hovered over them both must work itself
out.

A whistle shrilled from the road. Jap sprang up
with a strangled cry, as Wat Harlow came through
the gate. His face was stern.

"Bill allowed that this is where I'd find you, chatting your valuable time away," he chaffed. Then the
mask of his countenance broke into a grin.

"Is Bill in the office?" Jap's lips were so stiff he could
scarcely articulate.

"Sure he is," said Harlow cheerfully. "He wants
you to ramble down there."

"There's a hen on, Jap," he confided, after they had
taken leave of Flossy. "We'll try to hatch something
this time. I'm going to get in the game again. You

know the old saying: 'You musn't keep a good dog chained up.'"

"Well?" queried Jap, his thoughts springing space and picturing what Bill might be doing. Wat was discreetly silent until they had passed through town and were inside the office. Bill, pale and haggard, looked up from his desk. He extended the paper he was writing on. Jap took it without a word.

"WAT HARLOW FOR GOVERNOR!"

"How's that for a head?" he demanded. "If we're going into this thing, we might as well go with both feet."

He looked into Jap's face. Their eyes met. With one voice they cried:

"Ellis!"

"'When Harlow runs for governor,'" Jap quoted tremulously, "'you will boom him. Till then, nothing doing in the Halls of Justice.' Bill, Ellis was a prophet. He even knew that he wouldn't be in the game. Wat, we'll put you across this time."

"Yes, and it'll be a nasty fight," Wat returned, as Bill leaned over and picked nervously at the ears of the office cat. "We've got Bronson Jones to buck up against, in all political probability. He's almost sure of the nomination."

"Just who is Bronson Jones?" Jap asked. "Seems to me I ought to place him. He's been in the papers down in the southwestern part of the state a good deal."

"He's the smooth proposition that came back here a couple of years ago and bought back his old newspaper for his son and has managed up to the present time to keep his own name discreetly out of that same paper," vouchsafed Harlow. "He won't let it leak out till the psychological moment. He's the daddy of the split-hoofed imp of Satan that runs the Barton *Standard!*"

CHAPTER XVII

JAP threw his pencil impatiently on the desk.

"I can't get my thoughts running clear this morning," he said abruptly. "Every time I try to write, the pale face of little J. W. comes between me and the page."

"They're back from the city," Bill said uneasily. "I saw them coming from the train. I fully meant to tell you, Jap."

"I hope the specialist has quieted Flossy's fears." Jap ran his fingers through his loose red locks. "The boy is growing too fast. Why, look at the way he has shot up in the last year. Ellis told me that he ran up like a bean pole, the way I did, and just as thin. J. W. is exactly like him."

"And Ellis died at forty———"

"Don't, Bill," Jap choked. "I can't bear it." He walked to the door and gazed out into the hazy silver autumn air.

"This weather is like wine," he declared. "It will set the boy up, fine as a fiddle. You must remember, Bill, that Ellis impoverished his system by the life of hardship he was forced to endure while the town was

167

growing. The things he used to tell were humorous enough, the droll way he had of telling them. But they break our hearts when we think of them now, and know that it was that privation that killed him. It was bad enough here when I was a youngster, and that was luxury to what he had had. J. W. has not had such a handicap. Of course he was a delicate baby, but he certainly outgrew all that."

Bill was discreetly silent. He knew that Jap was only arguing with his fears. In the early summer, J. W. had been acutely ill, and as the heat progressed, he languished with headache and fever. In the end, Dr. Hall had counselled taking him to a noted specialist in the city.

"Better take a run up to Flossy's," Bill suggested. "You'll be better satisfied."

Jap took a copy of the *Herald* from the table and went out. All the way along Spring street he strove with his anxiety. Flossy met him on the porch. One glance was enough for Jap. He sat down, helpless, on the lower step.

"J. W. is tired out and asleep," said Flossy softly. "Come with me, Jap, down to the arbor. You remember the day that Ellis told you the truth about himself?"

Jap followed her beneath the grape trellis, stumbling clumsily. When they reached the arbor, with its bench and rustic table, she faced him, slender to attenuation.

"Jap," she said brokenly, "J. W. has tuberculosis in the worst form. His entire body is filled with it. He contracted it while we were with Ellis—and we never knew, never suspected——" Her voice broke. "Not even a miracle can prolong his life longer than spring. The doctors insisted on examining me, too. They say I have it, in incipiency, and my only chance of escape is to leave my boy to the care of others. Under the right conditions they say I have a fighting chance."

"You are sure that you have every advice?" Jap's voice was so hoarse that she looked up at him in alarm.

"Yes, Jap, but I knew it before. Months ago, even before he was so sick in the summer, I had a dream, and this was my dream: Ellis, with that beautiful smile that every one loved, was waiting out there at the gate, and I was hurrying to get the boy ready to go with him. I knew, when I awoke, that he was ready to wait our boy's coming. Oh, Jap, do you think that smile was for me, too?"

The look of agony in Jap's sensitive face was more than she could bear. She clutched his arm.

"Oh, Jap, pray—help me to pray that he was waiting for me, too. The time has been so long. I want to be with my boy to the last. You understand, Jap. I don't believe that words are needed."

He put his arms around her. He could not speak, but his head bent above hers and the hot tears dropped upon her brown hair, now streaked with gray.

"I have done the work he wanted me to do," she sobbed. "He wanted me to be a mother until you were on the plane he had planned. Like the butterfly whose day is done, Jap, I would go. I am so tired, and —boy, I have never ceased to long for Ellis. The world could not supply another soul like his."

"Flossy," Jap said in smothered tones, "I know. I have walked the floor for hours, missing him until I was almost frantic. But, little Mother, what is left to me if you go? Without you, I am drifting again."

"I would fear that, if I had never seen into the deeps of Isabel's nature. And to think that I once decried— but I didn't understand, Jap. When your mother came, there was a revelation. I don't fear for your future now. And when I knew this, I suddenly felt tired and old. I pray not to survive my boy."

The following morning brought the first fall rain. And then, for endless weeks, the leaden sky drooped over the world. Dreary depression and the penetrating chill of approaching winter filled the air. Only the un- wonted pressure of work kept the boys from brooding over the inevitable that would come with the spring- time. To relieve Flossy of all unnecessary burdens, Jap and Bill went to the hotel for their meals, but every evening one or the other went to sit with her. At length there came a time, late in November, when the office work was more than both of them could handle, and for several days the visits were interrupted.

"Flossy is sick," announced Bill, hanging his dripping raincoat behind the door. "I saw Pap just now, and he told me. He and his wife were there all night. He says that J. W. has been so bad off for a week, has had such bad spells at night, that Flossy has hardly slept, and yesterday she broke down and sent for Pap. He took Doc Hall along, and they are afraid she has pneumonia."

Jap threw his paper aside.

"Why didn't we know that J. W. was worse?" he demanded. "I sent some one to inquire every morning while we had the big rush on, and Flossy said that they were all right. I thought that she was going to take him to the mountains."

"I guess that she didn't know how sick he was," commented Bill. "Pap was to haul the trunks to-morrow, as Flossy told us. She wanted to start on Sunday so that you and I could go as far as Cliffton with her. She knew we were working overtime to get things cleaned up."

Jap put on his raincoat, for it was pouring a deluge.

"I will not be back if Flossy needs me," he said.

For three days and nights he hovered over the two sick-beds, while the wind soughed mournfully around the cottage, and the rain dripped, dripped, dripped, like tears against the wall outside. Neighbors and friends volunteered their services. Bill and Isabel came as often as was possible; but when all the others had gone, Jap kept his solemn vigil alone. On the afternoon of the fourth day, there was a sudden turn for the worse. Dr. Hall was hastily summoned. And then, all at once, without any seeming warning, it happened.

The last gasping breath faded from the body of Ellis's child, and as Jap leaned over to close the wide, staring eyes, he could hear the rasping breaths that rent Flossy's bosom, as she lay unconscious in the next room.

"With God's help we may pull her through," whispered Isabel, twining her arms around his neck. He turned stony eyes of grief upon her.

"If God helps, He will let her go with J. W. to meet Ellis," he said in a voice strained to breaking.

He drew the girl from the chamber of death, and sat down beside Flossy's bed. He caught one fluttering, fever-burned hand in his, and the restless muttering ceased. Then the eyes opened. They seemed to be looking not at Jap but above him.

"Ellis!" she cried, and slept.

"When she awakes, she will be better or——" Dr. Hall broke off, and went over to the window. "It's the crisis," he finished huskily.

Flossy, in her quiet, optimistic bravery, had made her place in the hearts of her townspeople. Isabel knelt beside her, watching Jap's face, with its unnatural calm, fearfully. She dared not speak. Bill stood awkwardly at the foot of the bed, his cap twirling uncertainly in his hand. His eyes shifted uneasily from the thin, white face on the pillow to the frozen features of Jap. A clock ticked loudly.

The thick gloom broke. A tiny linnet that Jap had given Flossy fluttered to the swing in its cage and burst, all at once, into song, and a vagrant sunbeam darted through the western clouds. Flossy opened her eyes.

"Jap," she gasped painfully, "is this the thing called Death, this uplift of joy?"

The doctor raised her in his arms and gave her a few sips of medicine. She was easier. She motioned Jap to bend closer.

"Is he gone?" she asked clearly. "Is my boy with his father?"

Jap kissed her forehead gently.

"He is with Ellis," he whispered.

"Then I thank You, great Giver of all Good," she cried happily, "for I can go now." She summoned Bill with her eyes.

"I want you to make the boy 'very proud of the men he was named for,' " she smiled. It was a smile of heavenly beauty, as the pure soul of Ellis Hinton's wife flew to join her loved ones.

CHAPTER XVIII

BILL and Isabel led Jap from the room as the doctor drew the sheet over Flossy's face. Together the three left the cottage. In dazed silence they walked past the row of modest homes until the business street was reached. Across Main street they went, in stony silence, the girl clinging to an arm of each of her escorts. In front of the elm-shaded residence of Tom Granger, now stark and bare in its late autumn undress, they paused. Isabel, unheedful of the passing crowd, threw her arms around Jap's neck and kissed him passionately. A moment he held her in his arms, his tearless eyes burning. And in her awakened woman's heart, she knew that he was looking through her, beholding the trio of adored ones whose influence had made his heart a fitting habitation for her own. And in that consciousness Isabel Granger experienced no twinge of jealousy.

Silently she walked up the brick-paved path to the stately old house, as Jap and Bill turned back toward Main street. When they reached the office, they locked the door behind them. With the mechanical action of automata, they climbed to their stools and threw the belated issue of the *Herald* into type.

"Bill, can you do it?" Jap asked at length.

"I'll do my best," Bill said huskily. And his tears wet the type as he set up a brief obituary notice.

The morning of the funeral broke clear and sunny, as fall days come. The air was clear and sounds echoed for long distances. It was a joyous new day, and yet a threnody swept through its music. Something of this Jap and Bill felt as they hurried to the house of Death. Judge Bowers met them at the door. His face was red and overcast. He shifted uneasily.

"I sent for you, because we have to fix things decently for Flossy."

"Decently?" echoed Bill.

"Why, yes. Ma and me got the caskets and all that. Everything's 'tended to, but the service. You know Flossy was a free-thinker, and never belonged to no church."

"Well, what of it?" Bill said shortly.

"We have got to get somebody to preach a sermon," asserted the Judge, his flaccid face showing real concern. "I don't see how we are going to manage it. It looks queer to ask anybody to preach over a non-professor."

"Why do it then?" Bill's tone was enigmatic, as he followed Jap into the little parlor where the effects of the Judge's work were apparent.

Side by side stood the caskets, each one holding a jewel more precious than any diadem. Jap sat down between them, dumb to the greetings of the friends who came for a last look at the two set faces, and there he sat until the afternoon. The room was half filled with people when the Judge aroused him by a sharp grip on his arm.

"Come on, Jap," he whispered huskily, "they have come for them."

"Who?" asked Jap, tonelessly.

"The hearses," said the Judge, his flabby cheeks trembling.

Jap walked outside and climbed into the carriage with Bill, and together they went to the church where Ellis had met his townsmen for the last time. It was the handsome new church whose claim on her brother's generosity had called forth from Flossy such righteous resentment. Mechanically the two young men followed the usher to the pew that had been set apart for them. Vaguely Jap smiled at Isabel as she passed him, clinging to the arm of her father. As in a dream, he followed her slender form as she took her accustomed place at the organ. Clutching the arm of the seat, he sat there, deaf, dumb and blind, until the wailing notes of the organ appraised him that the service was beginning.

He turned his head as a heavy, rolling sound reached him, and looked upon the most heart-shaking sight in the history of the town: two coffins traveling up the aisles to meet at the altar. Sick and faint, he turned his head away. Bill's arm crept around him, while Bill sobbed aloud.

Frozen to silence, Jap stared at the boxes containing all that linked him to his past. Stony-eyed, he gazed at the masses of flowers, casually admiring the gorgeous chrysanthemums and the pink glory of the carnations. He even read, with calm curiosity, the card of sympathy hanging from one of the floral offerings on Flossy's casket. Then he sank into blunt indifference until he was aroused by Bill's start.

He looked up dully. The minister was praying—and his prayer was for forgiveness for Flossy.

"She was a wanderer from grace," the ominous voice droned, "but Thou who didst forgive the thief on the cross wilt grant her mercy."

Bill clasped his hands fiercely over Jap's arm. His breath hissed through his set teeth. Jap sat upright, his gray eyes searching the face of the man of God, as he drawled through a flock of platitudes, promising in the end that on the last great day Flossy and her son would be called by the trump to arise, purified and forgiven.

Wiping his forehead complacently, he sat down.

Jap Herron arose to his feet and walked to the coffin of the only mother he had ever known. Facing the assembly, he said in low, clear tones:

"Friends of mine, friends of Flossy and her boy, and friends of Ellis Hinton, you have listened to this min-

ister. Now you must listen to me. I knew Flossy.
Some of you knew her, but none as I did. She had no
religion, he says. Flossy Hinton's life was a religion.
What is religion? Love, faith and works. Dare any
of you claim that she had not all of these? If such
soul as hers needs help to carry it through the ram-
parts of heaven, then God help all of you.

"She will not sleep until a trumpet calls her! No!
Alive and vital and everlasting, her soul is with us now.
Did Ellis Hinton sleep? He has never been away. He
has dwelt right here, in the hearts of all who loved him.
Friends, dry your eyes if you grieve for the sins of
Flossy."

Raising his hand above the casket, as if in benedic-
tion, and looking into the face beneath the glass, he said
brokenly:

"A saint she lived among us. In heaven she could be
no more."

The descending sun shot a ray of white light across
the church, as it sank below the opaque designs in the
gorgeous memorial window that flanked the choir. A
moment later it would be crimson, then purple, then
amber; but for an instant it filtered through pure, un-
tinted glass. Creeping stealthily, the white ray reached
the space in front of the altar and rested a moment
on the still face within the casket. To Jap it seemed
that the lips that had always smiled for him relaxed
into a smile of transcendent beauty. Entranced he

looked, forgetting all else.   Then the strength of his
young manhood crumbled.   The hinges of his knees
gave way, and he sank to the floor.

Bill sprang to his side and carried him to a seat.
Isabel, half distracted, started from her place at the
organ. As she passed, the white face in the coffin met
her eyes. She stopped. A tide of feeling swept her
back, back from Jap, whose limp form called her. The
song that Flossy had loved came singing to her lips.
Inspired in that moment, she stood beside the coffin and
sang, as never before, the words that had comforted
Flossy in her years of loneliness:

> "Somewhere the stars are shining,
>   Somewhere the song birds dwell.
> Cease then thy sad repining!
>   God lives, and all is well."

Her face was glorified. She sang to that silent one,
and to the world that had been hers. In a dream she
sang on, as the mother and her boy were taken from
her sight, sang on while the people silently departed.
"Somewhere, somewhere," she sang,

> "Beautiful isle of Somewhere,
>   Isle of the true, where we live anew,
> Beautiful isle of Somewhere."

Her voice broke as uncontrollable sobs rent her
slender body, and she sank against the shoulder of her

father and followed Bill from the church. Half-a-dozen kindly hands were carrying Jap outside.

The long line of carriages had already started on its way to the little plot of ground where two fern-lined graves awaited the loved ones of Ellis Hinton. The horses of the remaining carriage pawed the ground restlessly in the sharp November air.

"Better take him to his room in a hurry," Dr. Hall commanded. "The boy has been through too much. I was afraid of this."

"You can't take him to that dreary office," Isabel pleaded. "Papa, tell Dr. Hall what to do."

And, as always, she had her way. In the sunny south room above the library, with the shadows of the stark elms doing grotesque dances on the window panes, with Isabel and her mother hovering in tender solicitude over him, Jap Herron tossed for weeks in the delirium of fever, calling always for Flossy.

CHAPTER XIX

"Mr. Bowers wants to talk to you," Isabel said, smoothing Jap's limp hair from his haggard face. "He has been here every day for a week, and Mamma wouldn't hear to his bothering you, especially as you had concluded that you must talk to Bill about the office."

"Let him come," said Jap wearily.

The Judge tramped heavily into the bedroom.

"I want to talk to you about Flossy's affairs," he declared, dropping into a chair and blowing his nose.

Jap's face flushed, then paled. He lifted one thin hand to his eyes and leaned back in the pillows.

"I sent for Bill to meet me here and have Brent Roberts read Flossy's will."

"Why?" Jap's voice rasped with pain.

"You have been sick nigh a month," said the Judge, "and there's a power o' things that oughter be seen to, and Brent refused to read Flossy's will till you could hear it. I want to settle the bills."

Isabel slipped her arm around Jap's shoulder and glared at the Judge.

"You ought to be ashamed," she cried. "Jap is not strong enough to be bothered with business."

Jap put her aside gently and sat up.

"The Judge is right, sweetheart," he said. "I will not be tired with doing anything for—for her."

He covered his face with his hands. Bill entered softly. His brows lowered at sight of his father.

"What did you want with me and Roberts?" he queried shortly.

"It is all right, Bill," Jap said brokenly. "It will hurt whenever it comes, so let's get it done."

After the will was read Jap lay silent, the tears slipping down his cheeks, for Flossy's will gave all that she possessed to her son, Jap Herron. It was made the day after she knew that her own child was doomed to an early death.

They filed slowly from the room, even the Judge awed by the face of the boy.

The New Year had turned the corner when Jap was moved to the office. Little by little he grew back into harness. They did not talk of Flossy in those early days. It was not possible. One chill spring day, when the grass was greening, and the first blossoms were opening among the hyacinths on Ellis's grave, Jap walked with Bill to the cemetery. He bent above the dried wreaths with their faded ribbons, sodden and dinged by the winter's snows.

"Throw them away, Bill," he choked. "They are the tawdry tokens of mourning. I am trying to forget that mourning."

Bill gathered the dry bundles and carried them away. Coming back, he stood looking mournfully upon the muddy sod. Jap raised his eyes suddenly, and they gazed for a long minute into each other's hearts. Bill threw his hands over his eyes and cried aloud.

"Don't, Bill!" Jap's hand clutched him tightly. "For God's sake, help me to be a man!"

And forgetting the sodden grass, they knelt beside the grave and sobbed together in an abandon of grief. Boys they were, despite their years, and Flossy had been more to them than the mother whom youth is prone to take for granted. When the tempest of sorrow and desolation had spent itself they arose.

"It is done," said Jap, looking up into the sky where the stars were beginning to twinkle palely. "It had to be done. Now I can realize that they laid Flossy beneath the earth. But, please God, I can forget it. Now I know that she has left the beautiful shell behind. But, Bill," he touched the mound with his fingers, "Flossy has never been here, never for an instant."

"She is in heaven," said Bill reverently.

Jap laid his arm around Bill's shoulders.

"You don't believe that, Bill. You know better. Flossy is right with us, as Ellis has always been. Just as he has inspired us to develop his paper and his town, so she will stay with us, to create good and optimism and faith in ourselves. Bill, when those two wonderful people came into our lives, they came to stay.

Do you think Ellis and Flossy would get any joy out
of strumming on a harp and taking their own selfish
ease? No, Bill, that's all a mistake. They're working
right with us, and it's up to you and me to so wholly
reflect them that we will be to this town what they
have been to us. In any crisis in our lives, let us not
forget that Ellis and Flossy Hinton are not dead. We
may have need to remember it, Bill."

The next morning he climbed on his stool and took
the stick in his hand. Bill stopped at the door of
the composing room, something in Jap's attitude ar-
resting him.

"What are you going to do, Jap?"

"Get busy," declared Jap. "We have given out
enough plate. The *Herald* is going back on the job."

Bill felt a lump rise in his throat as he paused to
finger the copy on his hook.

"We have to get the drums beating," said Jap. "We
have to elect Wat Harlow governor, and, believe the
Barton *Standard,* we have some rough road to travel."

And the battle was on! Alone, the Bloomtown *Herald* tackled the job of making a governor. Watson
Harlow had been a familiar figure in state politics for
more than twenty years, but as gubernatorial timber
no one had ever regarded him seriously. His opponent,
on the other hand, was a fresh figure in the state, with
all the novelty of the unknown quantity about him.
It was an off year for the dominant party, both locally

and nationally, and the fight promised to be a compli-
cated one.

Week by week the battle raged between the types.
Little by little the country press began to get in the
fight. Not content with the picturesque drumming
of his own machine, Jap interested the city press in
the history of Wat Harlow, the "Lone Pine, of Integrity Absolute." This descriptive title was proclaimed
in and out of season during the months of battle,
both before and after the nomination of Harlow and
Jones. Jap invented a stinger for Bronson Jones. In
his past history, it was alleged, he had much that were
better concealed than revealed. Not the least of his
offenses was that he had assisted his father, a certain
P. D. Jones, in stealing red-hot cook-stoves from the
ruins of the Chicago fire. Jap so declared, and he
offered to prove that Jones had sold these same stoves
to their former owners, when they became cold. In one
instance, the victim was a widow who had lost everything, even her former mate, in the fire. And Jones
carried the title, "The Widow's Friend," for years.
All this was fun for the city dailies, and cartoons of
the "Lone Pine" being fed to the "Cook-Stove" alter-
nated with those of the pine falling upon the "Widow's
Friend" as he was about to sell a stove to the above-
mentioned widow.

The color came back to Jap's cheeks, and the battle
light flamed in his gray eyes. His one relaxation was

the tranquil hour with Isabel. Harlow, like an uneasy ghost, haunted the *Herald* office when he was not out storming the hustings. The Barton *Standard* continued to pry into Wat's past, while the *Herald* continued to lift the lid from the chest of Bronson's secret garments. Unfortunately, the *Standard* had played its big trump card in the congressional campaign. The vermilion handbill was once more dragged to light, but it worked like a boomerang, for several of Wat's own party workers had been caught red-handed in the act of attempting to operate a shameless graft game, in the name of the university. And Jap utilized the story to show that Wat was a man above party, a man in whose mind integrity was indeed absolute.

Argument grew red hot, every place but Bloomtown. There, there was no one to argue with. Bloomtown was one man for Harlow. Jones undertook to deliver one speech there, and that bright hour nearly became his last. After the good-natured raillery of the opening address, Jones plunged into the vitriolic explosion he had delivered at the various places he had spoken. For exactly ten minutes it lasted. By that time, Kelly Jones had reached Hollins's grocery store and gathered enough eggs to start a protest against the defamation of Wat Harlow's character. And the protest was proclaimed unanimous!

It was stated that there were no eggs on Bloomtown's breakfast table next morning, and no Sunday cakes.

"But," said the *Herald*, "if Bronson Jones wants any more hen-fruit, the housewives of Bloomtown will cheerfully sacrifice themselves in his behalf."

And so the months sped away until the grass had mossed the graves in the cemetery with lush beauty, and the three mounds were merged into one by the riotous growth of sweet alyssum, Flossy's best loved blossom. The summer waned. The autumn hasted, and chill winds whispered around the Lone Pine as the last sortie was made. Then Bloomtown pressed her hands to her throbbing breast and got ready for— Victory?

CHAPTER XX

BILL jumped from bed as the rattle of the latch announced the arrival of a visitor. Without waiting for the formality of more than a bathrobe, Rosy Raymond's last birthday gift to him, he bolted down the stairs and across the office. He flung the door open and disclosed the hazy features of Kelly Jones, peering at him through the November fog.

"What, ho! Kelly, what brings you to our door in the glooming?"

Kelly shook the rain from his slicker and came inside.

"Wife called me at three o'clock," he announced. "Had my breakfast and rid like hell to git to town early. I want to cast the fu'st vote for Wat for governor."

Bill yawned.

"You could have ridden more leisurely, and saved us a couple of hours' sleep," he complained. "There are at least a thousand voters of Bloomtown with that same laudable intention. Tom Granger has been missing since seven o'clock last night. It is believed that he is locked in the booth so that his vote will skin the rest."

188

Kelly looked ruefully back into the rain.

"I reckon that I will come in and set a while, that bein' the report."

"Any man found voting for Jones is to be lynched at sunset," declared Bill, pushing a chair forward.

"Reckon this'll be a big day for the Democrats," commented Kelly, stretching his feet across the table comfortably. " 'Tain't nothin' to keep 'em home, so they'll kill time, votin'. That's why I allus cussed my daddy for raisin' me a Democrat. Bein' as I am one, I've got to stick by and see the durn fools shuckin' corn while the Republicans are haulin' their grand-daddies in town to vote the Republicans in."

Bill retired to don a few garments and Jap tumbled from bed, for this was a big day in Bloomtown. Before six o'clock the roads were lined with vehicles, as for an Independence holiday. The county was coming in to help the town vote for her favorite son.

About noon Harlow came creeping up the alley and slipped in at the back door. He wore a slicker that he had borrowed from some constituent who was short. It hung sorrowfully about his knees. Bill remembered that in spike-tail coat and white necktie Wat Harlow looked enough like a governor to pass for one, but just now he resembled nothing so much as a draggled rooster. The stove in the little private office hissed and sputtered as he shook the rain from the coat.

"I thought that the only place that victory would

be complete would be the *Herald* office," he said, relaxing into a chair. "And if we are beat, I could meet it better here." He took a paper in his shaking hands and tried to read.

The rain poured in torrents, but Bloomtown cast her record vote—and not one scurrilous vote against him dropped into the ballot box. At sunset a wild yell proclaimed that Bloomtown had done her duty. It was now up to the rest of the state whether Wat Harlow, proclaimed from border to border as an honest man, would be its next governor. On his record as opposed to State University graft, he had once been elected to the legislature when the running was close. On that same record, as opposed to higher education, he was defeated for United States Congressman, and on that same record he was running for governor of his state.

The *Herald* office lighted up. All the big men of Bloomtown smoked the air blue, waiting for the returns. First good, then crushingly bad, they varied. By the tone of the operator's yell, the waiters guessed each bulletin. If he came silent, they all coughed and waited for some one to take the fatal slip of paper. The dawn was graying when they dispersed, with the issue still in doubt. It was late afternoon before they knew that Harlow was elected. Bill grinned joyously, for the first time since Rosy Raymond carried her heart to Barton and left it there.

"How many roosters have we?" he asked impishly, as he walked over to the telephone.

"Why?" queried Jap.

"I am going to 'phone Jones that we want to borrow all that he don't need," said Bill, taking the receiver from the hook.

"We done it!" yelled Kelly Jones, slapping his slouch hat against the door. "And I'm goin' over to Barton and git on the hell-firedest drunk that that jay town ever seen. Whoopee!" And off he set at a run to catch the local freight.

About half of Bloomtown seemed inspired with the same spirit, and the freight pulled out amid wild yells of joy. Several of the most agile among the jubilant ones draped the box cars with strips of faded, soggy bunting, and Harlow's picture adorned the cow-catcher. The yelling, that had been discontinued for economic reasons, was resumed in raucous chorus as the train rolled into Barton to celebrate Harlow's victory in Jones's town.

The Bloomtown *Herald* did itself proud that week. A mammoth picture of the Lone Pine stood forth on the front page. Around it fluttered one hundred flags. Every page sported roosters and flags in each available space, between local readers and editorial paragraphs. It was a thing of beauty and a joy forever—at least to Wat Harlow. One other cut found place at the bottom of the editorial page. Bill did not forget to boomerang

Wilfred Jones by reprinting the weeping angel. For a week there were bonfires every night, and a number of Bloomtown's citizens sought to lighten Barton's woes by buying fire-water there. Wat swelled until he looked more like a corpulent oak than a lone pine.

"My house is yours," he cried, alternately wringing Jap and Bill by their weary hands. He had come across once more from his headquarters in the Court House to make sure his appreciation was understood. Jap smiled wanly as the village band followed him with its intermittent serenade.

Bloomtown had long since outgrown the village class; but not a drum nor a horn had encroached upon the old traditions of that band. Mike Hawkins was far too conservative to permit innovation, and as there was no provision for retiring the bandmaster on half pay, the problem of dividing nothing in half having as yet been unsolved, Mike continued to hold the job. All day the band had been vibrating between the Court House and the *Herald* office, having delivered ten serenades at each side of Main street, for it was understood that the *Herald* shared the victory with Harlow. As the Governor-elect retreated to the other side of the street, the band at his heels, Bill groaned aloud.

"I wish that that bunch of musicians had had more confidence that Wat was going to get it," he sighed, "so that they could have learned one tune good."

Kelly Jones was capering down the street. Kelly

had absorbed enough of Barton booze to make him believe he owned the half of Bloomtown that did not belong to Wat Harlow. He had been having what Bill described as "one large, full time." As he came in sight, Bill's brow darkened.

"I've been afraid that Kelly would burst and catch fire," he said morosely, "and now, by jolly, I wish he would. It's funny how much your good friends will get in your way when they pair off with John Barleycorn. Kelly is certainly one ding-buster when he is lit up."

Jap leaned from the door to watch the procession that had formed for the purpose of escorting Wat Harlow to the station.

"Kelly's time is wrinkling," he laughed. "Here comes Mrs. Kelly Jones, with worriment on her brow."

Bill ran his inky fingers through his hair. Something was troubling him.

"Jap," he said as he walked toward the door of the composing room, "that skunk of a Jones——"

"Who? Kelly?"

"Oh, no." Bill wheeled, and his face was deadly earnest. "Kelly's not a skunk, even when he has soaked up all the rotgut in Barton. But I had Kelly Jones in the back of my head, just the same, when I mentioned the honorable Editor of the Barton *Standard*. It's getting under my skin, Jap, the way he has of tempting these Bloomtown fools over to his filthy village to get the booze we won't let 'em have at home,

and then holding them up to ridicule when they make
asses of themselves."

"It's one of the angles of this problem that I haven't
figured out yet," Jap said earnestly. "Do you think
it would do any good to go gunning for Jones?"

"I've thought of that possibility several times," and
Bill's tone was not entirely humorous.

Jap shoved his stool to the case. As he climbed upon
it, he sighed uneasily. It had been sixteen months since
Wilfred Jones turned the neat trick that left Bill disconsolate, and still the venom lingered in the bereft
boy's heart. To Jap, with his standard of womanhood
established by Flossy and Isabel, the thing was mon-
strous, inconceivable. And yet it was a fact to be
faced.

"We'll have to get busy, Bill," he said. "We've got
enough job work on the hooks to keep us up till midnight for a week. We haven't done a thing the last
month but elect Wat Harlow."

"I hope to grab he won't run for another office till I
have six sons to help me," Bill snorted.

Jap heaved a sudden sigh of relief.

"Looking out again, Bill?" he asked, jerking his
thumb in the direction of the vacant photograph frame
above Bill's case.

CHAPTER XXI

I⊤ was the day after Thanksgiving. Bill was twirling the chambers of his revolver around. His face was grim. Jap halted in the door of their bedroom.

"Going gunning for Jones?" he asked lightly.

Bill turned, and the black look on his face startled Jap.

"I am," he said deliberately, "and I will come back to jail or in my coffin."

Jap caught the revolver from his hand.

"Bill," he said sharply, "wake up!"

Bill threw a letter to him, and continued his hasty toilet. Jap read:

"Dear Will,—

"Come to me. I am almost crazy. Wilfred accused me of giving you information against his father that beat him in the election, and he struck me in the mouth. He said he only married me to spite you, and he hates me. I will meet you at the section house, where the train slows up for the switch, at six o'clock. I want you to take me away, I don't care where. I don't love anybody but you, and I can't live with Wilfred another night. I don't care whether anybody ever speaks to me again, if you will take me and love me.

"Your distracted ROSALIE."

Jap stared at the note as if it had been a snake-tressed Medusa that turned him to stone. He stood rigid and paralyzed as Bill said, deadly calm:

"I am going to Barton, and I am going to shoot that dog."

"And after that?" Jap's voice was toneless.

"After that!" Bill broke out fiercely. "After that, what more?"

Jap drew Bill around to face him. Rivers of fire seemed suddenly to course through his body, and an unprecedented rage burned up within him.

"You are not going to Barton, and you are not going to meet that foolish light-o'-love at the section house," he said sternly.

"Who will stop me? Not you, Jap, for even if an angel from heaven tried to bar my way, I would brush it aside. I wanted to kill him when he stole her away and——"

Jap shook him angrily.

"No one stole her, Bill. Have you forgotten the insolent, flippant letter she wrote you?"

Bill shook Jap's hand from his shoulder.

"It's no use, Jap. I am going to kill him!"

Jap set his teeth and his gray eyes blazed as he gripped Bill's arms and shoved him into a chair.

"I will have you locked up, you foolish hot-head," he exclaimed, "and give Wilfred Jones a few hours to consider his attitude toward his wife. She *is* his wife, Bill, and all your heroics won't gloss that fact from sight. Do you want to hang, because you were a damned fool? I can consider a romantic close to your career, but not as an intruder in another man's home —no matter how great your feeling of injustice. Rosy was not a child when she married Wilfred Jones."

"But he struck her," gulped Bill.

"I have known times," declared Jap vehemently, "when, if I had been of the fibre of Wilfred Jones, I would have felt satisfaction in thrashing Rosy Raymond. Not having been Jones, I had to content myself with kicking the furniture around. I don't want to rile you, Bill, but I rather think there are two sides to this story, and I want to hear both sides. If it is proven that Jones has mistreated Rosy brutally, I will hold him while you give him the licking he deserves. More than that, I will help Rosy to get a divorce. Isn't that fair enough, Bill? What is revenge upon a dead body, especially if you expiate that revenge on the gallows? Tell me, who profits? For the woman, disgrace. For you—— Humph! the only one who comes out of it honorably is the dead man, Jones."

Bill glowered at him.

"You had no mother, Bill, because she died when she gave you to the world. I had no mother, because Providence gave me where I was a burden. But God gave both of us a mother. Bill, before you go any farther with this adventure—misadventure—I want you to kneel with me before Flossy's picture and ask for her approval and her blessing. Because, Bill, brother, she knows. And what do you suppose will be her counsel? What would Flossy want you to do?"

He took the photograph from the table and held it out to Bill. The brown eyes remained downcast. The hands opened and closed spasmodically. Jap lowered the picture so that Bill's eyes could not choose but meet the loved face. A great, gulping sob shook him, and he dashed into the other room and slammed the door. Jap's tense features relaxed into a smile. He knew that Flossy had won.

"Will you let me go to Barton instead of you?" he asked through the closed door. There was no reply, and he turned the knob. Bill was staring stolidly from the window. "I won't carry healing oil if the case doesn't call for it," he insisted. "You will believe me, boy?"

"It's your job," Bill said, in smothered, tear-drenched tones.

"I can just make the 5:20," said Jap, as he caught up his hat and overcoat from the foot of the bed where he had flung them. Then he hurried to the station, with Rosy's foolish letter in his pocket.

Without looking to right or left he boarded the train that would have carried Bill to his love tryst. Already the evening shadows were beginning to settle, and it was almost dark when the local train ran into the siding to permit the east-bound special to pass. He stood on the steps of the rear coach as the wheels crunched with the stopping of the train. Then he dropped quietly to the ground. The special, that was wont to throw dust in the eyes of both Bloomtown and Barton, came thundering by, and the friendly local took up its westward journey.

Jap hurried over to the cloaked figure that crouched in the shadow of the little section house. Rosy crept out quickly, but retreated with a cry of alarm when she saw that Jap, and not Bill, was coming to meet her. He caught her by the arm and drew her into the light of an electric bulb that glowed above the section boss's door. Scanning her silly face for a moment, he said sharply:

"So you lied to Bill! There is no mark of a blow on your face."

"He—he did push me," she sobbed. "And I don't love him, anyway. It was your fault that I ran away with Wilfred."

"My fault?" echoed Jap.

"Yes," she said, and her tone rasped with cruel spite.

"What girl wants to have her sweetheart only half hers? Jap Herron only had to twist his thumb, and Bill would run like a foolish girl. I wanted a whole man or none."

"Seems that you got one," commented Jap, "and don't appreciate him. Now, Rosy, if you think you are going to ruin three lives by starting this kind of a play, I am going to undeceive you. I am going to take you home and look into this affair."

"I won't go!" she screamed. "He would kill me."

"What did you do?" demanded Jap, holding her tightly.

"I wrote him a note that I had run away with Bill," she confessed sullenly.

For the first time Jap became conscious of the suitcase at her feet. His grip on her arm tightened until she cried with pain.

"You idiotic little fool," he ground between his teeth. "Where is your husband?"

"He went to the city this morning. He said he'd come home on the local if he got through his business in time. Otherwise he wouldn't come till the midnight train. I thought Bill could get a rig and drive to Faber. I thought he could take me away somehow before Wilfred got the news."

"News? Great God!" cried Jap. "And such as you could win the golden heart of Bill Bowers! Come with me. If your husband takes the late train, there is still time to destroy that note. If he is already at home——"

"He'd go to the office first, anyway," Rosy cried. "But I don't want to go home."

"You're going home, no matter what the consequences," Jap told her. "And if you ever attempt to communicate with Bill again, I will have you put in an asylum. You are not capable of going through life sensibly."

He walked her rapidly up the railroad track and through the streets that lay between the business part of Barton and her own pretty home. On the corner opposite the house he stopped, while she ran across the street in terror and rushed up the steps. She had told him that if all was yet well, she would appear at the window. As he stood there, his eyes glued on the great square of glass, some one touched him on the arm. He turned. It was Wilfred Jones.

"Well, Daddy-long-legs," he said brusquely. "You think you turned a pretty trick. Well, it was a fair fight, and I'm all over it."

Jap shook his hand mechanically, his eyes seeking the window from which Rosy was peering.

"Tell Bill that bygones must be bygones," Jones continued, "for we want to get the two papers together on the main issue. The old man will come in on the senatorship on the strength of his race for governor. And I want to tell you a secret that makes me very happy

—and will make Bill feel different. The doctor has just told me that these queer spells and moods that Rosalie has been having lately mean—Jap, do you understand? I will be a father before summer!"

Jap wrung Jones's hand, a whirl of fancies going through his head. As he sought for suitable words of congratulation, a boy ran up.

"I been chasin' all over town ahuntin' for you, Mr. Herron," he said breathlessly. "I got a telegram for you."

Trembling with dread, Jap tore it open and read:

"*Come home at once. Your sister Agnesia is here.*　　　　Bill."

CHAPTER XXII

THE streets were deserted as Jap came from the station. In his state of mind, he did not reflect on the oddity of this circumstance. But had he reflected, the condition of traffic congestion at the corner near Blanke's drug store and the further congestion in front of the bank would have enlightened him. All the business men of Bloomtown, who had rushed to the *Herald* office with important advertisements or news items, were reluctantly giving place to those who had discovered a sudden want of letter-heads.

The telegraph office at Bloomtown was no secret repository, and in less than ten minutes after Bill had telegraphed Jap to hurry home the whole street knew that the beautiful vision that arrived on the 5:20 was Jap Herron's sister, Agnesia. And forthwith traffic filed that way.

The vision arose as Jap entered the front door, and waited until he came into the private office. It was apparent that Bill had played host, to the limit of his meager resources. Agnesia's hat and fur-trimmed coat lay on the table of exchanges.

"Well, Jappie," she laughed in silvery tones, "how long you are!"

He took her little ringed hands in his and looked at her silently. Agnesia was the beauty of the family. Her golden curls fluffed bewitchingly about her face and her wide blue eyes smiled affectionately.

"You are grown, too, Aggie. I have been thinking of you as a very little——"

"Mercy!" she broke in. "Please, Jappie, don't drag that awful name to light. When I went to the new home, they mercifully killed Agnesia. I have been Mabelle Hastings so long that I had almost forgotten Aggie Herron. I gave that hideous name to your friend," she flung a gold-flashed smile at Bill, "because you had no sister Mabelle in the old days. Our folks made a bad selection of names for their progeny. And why Jasper? Why didn't they put the James first? It sounds so much more human."

"Not a bit of it!" declared Bill. "What is there about James? This town had to have its Jap Herron. No substitute would have made good."

She slipped a glance through her long lashes at Bill.

"I called him 'Jappie,'" she confided. "I was a lisping baby and couldn't say 'Jasper.' Dear old Jappie, how he slaved for me! And I was a tyrant, demanding service every minute of the day."

Jap's face clouded. "Aggie is a bigbug now," came surging into his memory, as a wizened face obtruded itself between the laughing eyes of his sister and his own. The girl noted the swift change. She took his hand, her voice quivering with appeal.

"I know what you are thinking about," she said. "But I could not help it, Jappie. We don't have to keep up the pretense before Mr. Bowers. He knows the worst, I take it. Jappie, you may not remember, but when Mrs. Hastings adopted me, my mother had reported that she would either turn me out or give me to the county. Afterward my foster-mother took me away from Happy Hollow when she saw that our mother was bringing disgrace on all of us. She sacrificed her home and moved far enough away so that no smirch could come to me. You don't know, brother, and I would never want you to know the dreadful things she did. I had not heard from her since she married that drunken brute, until she came to the house one hot day. When she found no one at home, she laid down on the porch and went to sleep, drunk and unspeakably filthy. She was there when we returned with a party of friends. Can you imagine it, Jappie?"

Jap nodded his head slowly.

"Mrs. Hastings had her taken out of town, and told her if she came there again she would have her put in an asylum for drunkards. After that she threatened to descend upon Fanny Maud. Fanny could not afford to have her career spoiled. Perhaps we were cruel. I read the scorching letter you wrote to Fanny after her—after mother's death. But Fanny was not angry with you, and—and she was willing to have me come to you now. Next spring she will graduate in vocal music from the highest university in the country, and then she goes to Paris to study under the artists there. Jappie, she has made a large part of it, herself, teaching and singing in the church choir, and studying whenever she had enough money ahead. At last Uncle Francis died and left her a snug little sum, and she went to New York, where they say her voice is a wonder. We should be proud of her. She wants you to come with me in June to hear her sing when she graduates."

Jap stared at the floor. She laid her hand coaxingly on his shoulder.

"Of course Jap will go!" Bill's brown eyes were glowing. Jap looked across at him in astonishment and wonder. His brain reeled. The day had been too full.

"And you?" the girl queried, smiling into those dancing brown eyes.

"We can't both go at once," he blurted. "The paper has to come out on time."

She arose and wandered through the rooms that occupied the lower floor of the building, stepping from a hasty and uncomprehending glance at the press room and the composing room to dwell with critical eye on the big, bare office.

"You need a little fixing up," she commented. "You should have a nice rug and shades, and a roll-top desk and swivel chair."

"So we should," lamented Bill, looking around with an air of disapproval. "But not having anybody to tell us——" He stopped short, embarrassed.

"I guess that I will have to keep house for Jappie, and boss the office too. That is, if you want me, Jappie," she appealed. "Mrs. Hastings died last March, and I have been with Fanny ever since. My foster-mother left me well provided for. I won't be a burden, Jappie," she cried. "We have all made good. We must rejoice together."

Bill was half way across the office in his excitement.

"You can take Flossy's house," he burst out. "It's ready any time, because Pap had it completely over-hauled after the tenants moved out. It's the only ready-furnished house in Bloomtown and——" His voice lowered and there was a note of wistfulness in it. "Jap, Flossy would be so happy!"

Jap surveyed his erstwhile desperate friend with a gleam of merriment. As yet, Bill did not know but that his sacrificing partner was a fugitive from the law. He had not even remembered to ask about the well-being of Wilfred Jones and his wife.

"Perhaps Aggie—Mabelle," he hastily corrected, "is just joking. She would hardly like to bury herself in this little town after New York. There would be so little to compensate."

"Oh, I don't fear that I will regret New York," said Mabelle, letting her blue eyes dwell on Bill's ingenuous countenance for a throbbing moment. "Really, Jappie, there's nothing to regret."

Bill's heart turned over twice. His face was appealing. He met Jap's dancing eyes defiantly.

"Well," said Jap, "you might get the keys and show the cottage to Ag—Mabelle, and see how much enthusiasm it provokes. Perhaps it would make a better first impression by electric light. Here, put an extra bulb in your pocket, if one happens to be missing," and he drew out the table drawer, where many things lay hidden.

Bill was helping Mabelle on with her coat, his well-set body charged with electricity that was strangely illuminating to Jap. As the two left the office, a few minutes later, a teasing voice called after them:

"Remember, Bill, that you took on a pile of orders this evening, and we were loaded to the guards with job work already."

CHAPTER XXIII

JAP looked up as a shadow fell across the door of the composing room.

"Well," he queried quizzically, "what about it?"

"Well," Bill repeated, drawing the girl into the room after him, "Mabelle thinks that the cottage needs a bathroom and about a wagon load of plumbing, besides paint and paper. Otherwise, it's all right."

Mabelle slipped past him and approached the case. Standing on tiptoe beside the high stool, she laid a hand coaxingly on the strong, angular shoulder.

"Now, Jappie, boy, iron out that worry-frown. I am going to do the fixing up myself. It shan't cost you a cent."

"No!" Jap exploded.

"Now, dear boy, forget your pride. I have lots and lots of money, and this is to be my home."

"The firm is not insolvent," suggested Bill.

"It isn't a matter for the firm," Jap said gravely. "The cottage belongs to me, and we can't allow our finances to get mixed. I'm willing to have you put in all the repairs that I can afford."

His mind reverted to Flossy, happy and clean without a bathroom.

"Let me take a mortgage on the property for whatever the work costs," Mabelle pleaded, her lips puckering irresistibly.

Jap descended from the stool and caught her in his arms. Somehow she had, all at once, become his baby sister again. The episode of the straw stack loomed before him. She had puckered her lips just like that when she fled to him for protection. With little coquettish touches, she slipped one arm around his neck, while she smoothed his red locks gently. Bill, looking on, was overcome by an unaccountable restlessness.

"What a pity Isabel isn't home!" he blurted. And Bill never knew why he had recourse to Isabel at that moment. The observation bore the desired fruit. Mabelle freed herself from her brother's embrace, with the pained exclamation:

"Isabel not at home! Oh, Jappie, I have just been waiting for you to tell me about her. Ever since we read in the paper—and the one little reference to her in your letter to Fanny——"

She stopped, her blue eyes filling with tears.

"They went away just after the election was over," Bill explained. "Iz wouldn't leave Jap while the thing was in doubt, not even for her mother."

"I don't think that's quite square," Jap interposed. "Mrs. Granger didn't want to go at all, and only consented when Dr. Hall told her how ill Isabel was. The rest of us knew that Mrs. Granger couldn't live through another winter here; but he had to make Isabel's poor health the pretext when he sent them to Florida for the cold weather."

"Is she—is she seriously sick?" Mabelle asked tremulously. "The mother, I mean."

"It's a desperate hope, a kind of last resort," Bill vouchsafed. "I heard Doc Hall talking to Tom Granger in the bank, the morning before they left. He said he didn't want to scare him, but he wanted to prepare him for the worst, I thought."

"I'm sure if Isabel were at home, she'd insist on your coming right to her," Jap said slowly. "Bill and I have been bunking together up there," he jerked his thumb in the direction of the ceiling. "We have a bedroom and a little combination living-room, dressing-room and library. The library's Bill's part. We take our meals at the hotel, down in the next block. The hotel isn't bad for a town of this size."

"Oh, I've already met the hotel," Mabelle laughed. "Bill—Mr. Bowers took me there to dinner this evening while we were waiting for you to come home."

"Aw, chuck that 'Mr. Bowers,' " Bill interrupted. "I'm plain Bill to everybody in this town, and I guess Jap's sister can call me that."

"The hotel, as I was saying," Jap resumed, "will have to take care of you for the present till you can get a bathroom attachment for the cottage. It'll probably be lonely for you, just at first."

"I'll see to it that Mabelle meets all the best people in town," Bill offered.

The temporary housing problem settled, they returned to the discussion of repairs necessary and repairs superfluous. After two hours of parley, Jap consented to let his energetic sister work her will on Flossy's cottage. It was after midnight when the girl had been established in her room at the hotel, and Jap and Bill tumbled into bed. The shank of that night had wrought miracles for unsuspecting Bloomtown. A vision of blue eyes, red lips and golden tresses kept floating through Bill's dreams, a vision that bore not the least resemblance to Rosy Raymond. Meanwhile Jap stalked through one dream controversy after another with plumbers, painters and the other defilers of Flossy's home.

By noon on Monday Mabelle had Bloomtown by the ears, and by the end of the week it was all up with Bill. Jap had to hire a boy to help get out the *Herald*. It consumed all of Bill's time threatening and cajoling merchants into the prompt delivery of supplies, and seeing to it that the workmen were on the job when Mabelle arrived at the cottage in the morning. Bloomtown carpenters, paper hangers and plumbers usually took their own sweet time. They had a great awakening when Mabelle employed them. With Bill to pour oil on the troubled waters, strikes were narrowly averted.

One morning, soon after the radiant one arrived, Kelly Jones wandered into the office, where a lively dispute with the boss plumber was under way. In ten minutes, Kelly had fallen a victim to the little tyrant.

" 'Tain't no use talkin' about her gittin' along without a cellar," he confided to Jap. "I'll dig it myself, and that'll save all this row about how the pipes is got to run. I ain't got nothin' much to do, now the corn's all in. And it's lucky we ain't had a hard freeze. The ground's fine for diggin'," and the following morning he was on the job.

For two months Bloomtown was demoralized. A cellar made possible a furnace, and the elimination of stoves called for a fireplace in the living-room, a fireplace framed in by soft blue and yellow tiles. One by one Mabelle added her receipted bills to the packet of documents that would go into the making of that mortgage on Jap's property. One by one the housewives of Bloomtown demanded of their paralyzed husbands bathrooms, cellars, furnaces, tiled fireplaces.

At last the agony was over. A load of furniture had arrived from the city, and Bill, as usual, left his stickful of type and hastened to superintend the transfer of it from the freight depot to the cottage. The evening shadows were lengthening in the office when he returned. Jap had gone up-stairs to get out a rush order on the job press, and there was a little commotion on the stairway just before Bill presented himself, his brown eyes full of trouble. Jap looked at him, and his heart sank. Had it come to this? Mabelle, in spite of her scanty years, was older than Bill. She must have known. The whole town knew.

"For goodness' sake, Bill, don't pi this galley," he shouted, bending over the imposing stone. "Look where you're going. I wish that Mabelle would wake to the fact that you have a half-hearted interest in this office. She thinks you have nothing to do but keep tagging on her errands."

The office cat rubbed her sleek side against Bill's leg.

"Get out and let me alone!" he screamed, jumping with nervous irritation.

"Don't do that, Bill," Jap said firmly. "What's the matter with you, anyway? You are as pernickety as a setting hen, as Kelly said yesterday. When even Kelly begins to notice your aberrations it's time for you to get a wake-up. Are you sick? Have things gone wrong?"

Bill walked over to the window and ran his thumb down the pane of glass absently.

"Jap, have you that mortgage handy—all that business that Mabelle gave you?"

Jap went to the safe and took out the packet of papers.

"Why?" he asked, as he glanced through the long list of items. "Has my sister thought of anything else she absolutely needs? In another week, I'll owe her more than the cottage is worth."

Bill took the documents gingerly. His mobile face flamed.

"I—I—want to take up the deeds," he stammered.

Jap whirled to face him.

"You see," stuttered Bill, "I—that is, we—Mabelle and I, we——"

Jap sprang forward, lithe as a panther, and caught Bill by the arm. Drawing him to the light, he looked full in the embarrassed face.

"Where is she?" he shouted. "Where is that sister of mine? Where is she hiding?"

The girl came from the dark hall, her eyes defiant, her head set with charming insolence on one side. Jap struggled with his self-possession an instant. Then a great, gurgling laugh shook his shoulders as he gathered the pair into his long arms.

"Golly Haggins!" the expletive of his boyhood leaped to his lips, "I'm glad the agony is over. Now perhaps we will be able to get the *Herald* to our subscribers on time."

CHAPTER XXIV

"Tom Granger got a telegram," announced Bill, coming into the office one morning early in April. "He wants to see you at once, Jap."

Jap's face blanched. He looked dumbly at Bill.

"No, it's not her," Bill hastened to say. "It's her mother."

Jap stumbled awkwardly up the walk to the Granger home. The letters from Isabel had been far from reassuring, and only the previous day Dr. Hall had sounded a warning that the care of the invalid was too much for the girl, taxed as she was in both mind and body. Into Jap's consciousness there crept the thought that she had never fully recovered from those terrible weeks when she hovered over him.

Tom Granger met him at the door. His eyes were red with weeping. He drew Jap into the parlor and gave him two telegrams.

"This came at midnight," he said brokenly. Jap read:

"Mother sinking. Come. Isabel."

"And this just arrived," Granger choked, as the fatal words met Jap's eye:

"Mother dying. Come. Bring Jap. ISABEL."

"The train leaves in half an hour. I don't have to ask you anything, my boy."

Jap turned and hastened away. He did not weaken Granger's feeble strength with words of sympathy.

It was the afternoon of the second day when the two stood with Isabel at the foot of the bed. Alice Granger lifted her heavy lids, and a gleam of recognition shone in her eyes. Swiftly those two, the husband and the child, drew near, eager for any word that might pass the stiffening lips. Jap stood looking sorrowfully down on her as they knelt at her side.

"Jap," she whispered, "you, too," and her feeble fingers drew him.

With a choked sob he knelt beside Isabel. The mother fumbled with the covers until her hand, icy cold, touched his. Instantly his firm, strong hand closed over it. She smiled and murmured:

"Tom. Isabel."

They leaned over her in a panic of fear.

"Isabel's hand," she breathed, and placed the two hands together. "Tom, there is time," she whispered; "I want——" She sank helpless.

"I know what you would say," cried Granger, the tears streaming down his face. "You want him to be our son before—before you say good-bye."

A flash of joy illumined her thin face. She sighed contentedly.

A minister was hastily summoned, and a half hour later Isabel sobbed her grief in the arms of her husband, as they stood awaiting the coming of the Death Angel.

"It made such a difference in her feeling toward you, your illness at our house," Tom said, looking down upon her closed eyes and fluttering lips. "She never understood you, and in her quiet way she was always reserving judgment, when I used to talk so much about you. A mother finds it hard to think any man is the right one for her only child, and she was so dependent on Isabel. She hadn't any doubts, after she saw you in that dreadful fever, with all your soul laid bare to us. She knew Isabel would be safe, and after that she stopped worrying."

A grim hand caught at Jap's throat, as Tom sank on his knees and buried his face in the pillow to smother his sobs. Into his memory there came the words of Flossy: "When your mother came, there was a revelation. I don't fear for your future now. And when I knew this, Jap, I suddenly felt tired and old."

Flossy had clung to life until he had found the woman who could take her place. Then, all at once, she let go. And now Alice Granger, an invalid for twenty-three years, had relaxed her feeble hold on life when she knew that her child was in safe and gentle hands. Must Death forever draw its grim fingers between him and his happiness? He looked at his bride, fragile as a spring flower, and a great fear rushed over him.

Dumb, he stood there, stroking Isabel's hair with futile caresses.

At last the glazing eyes opened, and Alice Granger said faintly:

"Tom, not alone."

"Not alone?" he cried in anguish. "Always alone without you, Alice."

She only smiled—and then she fell asleep.

It was a strange wedding journey. Between the half-crazed father and the exhausted wife, Jap was taxed to the uttermost. Isabel, for once helpless, lay white and silent in the compartment, too weak to do more than cling to her one tower of strength, while Tom Granger rent Jap's sympathetic heart with his unreasoning grief. At length nature demanded her own; from sheer exhaustion they slept. Jap left them alone and stood out on the platform between the coaches.

"Is my life always to hold grief?" he queried of his soul. A throb of fear tore at his consciousness. Isabel's death-white face arose before him.

"No!" he cried fiercely, "there is a God. He will not take all from me."

He went back into the car and, kneeling beside his sleeping wife, prayed madly to his God for mercy.

The grasses were green along the tracks, and the blue violets lifted their rain-washed faces as the familiar stations loomed in sight near the journey's end. At the last station below Bloomtown, Bill and Dr. Hall entered the sleeper.

"We have everything arranged," Dr. Hall said to Jap, while Bill fought with his tears. "Isabel Granger has gone through too much to stand the harrowing experience of a funeral. The carriages are waiting, and it has all been attended to at the cemetery. We'll just have a short service out there, and I want you to keep her in the carriage with you. Bill and I did things with a high hand, but it had to be so. I wouldn't risk having the girl look into her mother's grave. She couldn't stand it."

The platform was crowded with friends, and Tom Granger was responding to sympathetic greetings with tears he did not try to hold. Jap half carried Isabel to the nearest carriage, and Dr. Hall took his place with them. Bill had hurried to meet Mabelle, who tactfully drew Tom Granger into the second carriage, in which the minister sat waiting. In a dream the well known landmarks of Bloomtown passed before Jap's eyes. There was the quick jolt that marked the crossing of the railroad tracks, and then the cool green of the cemetery came into view.

While the brief service was read, Jap held Isabel tight to his aching breast. His eyes wandered away beyond the yellow mound of earth, and in the hazy distance he saw his City of Hope. The young grass smiled above the mounds that held the empty shells of those he had loved, the first in all the world who had loved him. On Flossy's straight white shaft he read "I Hope." That was all.

After the slow cortège had moved its way back to town, Mabelle left the carriage and approached her brother. Bill, with his face frankly tear-stained, was beside her. The coachman had descended from his box, and was opening the door.

"Let me take her—let me take your sweetheart to our cottage," she pleaded. Leaning past him, she took one of Isabel's black-gloved hands. "Dear, I am Jappie's sister. I want to have you with me until you are better."

Tom Granger sat up and leaned out of the carriage, so that all could hear him.

"Jap is coming home with us," he said. "He is my son. He was married to Isabel just before her mother left us."

And it was thus that after well-nigh three years of waiting Bloomtown celebrated the long-expected happiness of her best loved son.

CHAPTER XXV

IsABEL had a long, lingering illness. It was plainly impossible for Jap and Mabelle to go to New York to see Fanny Maud make her debut. Mabelle had been a ministering angel, so faithful in her care of the invalid that an unreasoning jealousy blotted the grin of contentment from Bill's face as he uncomplainingly took the brunt of work at the office. Jap was too abstracted to notice the Associate Editor's woe. One day, when rosy June was just bursting its buds, he glanced hurriedly through the columns of the *Herald*, still damp from the press. He started, and looked keenly at Bill. Second column, first page, under a double head that reduced the day's political sensation to minor importance, he read:

"Our Neighbor Rejoices; Twins Come to the Editor of the Barton Standard."

"Whew!" he whistled. Bill looked up. The red flew to his cheeks.

"Both boys," he commented, folding papers rapidly. "Be in line for pages, when old Brons lands in the Halls of Justice."

Jap hurried home to tell the news. Isabel, still pale

and weak, was lying in the hammock on the screened porch. She laughed, her old merry laugh, when Jap told her of Rosy Raymond's achievement. Mabelle tossed her yellow curls.

"Well, I don't think she was worrying Bill," she snapped.

"There is no heavier blow to romance than twins," Jap said.

"Maybe she will call them Jap and Bill," crisped Mabelle, and stopped short when her brother walked abruptly to the other end of the porch.

"I hope that it won't fluster you to know that Bill and I are going to be married before Fanny Maud leaves for Europe," she flung at him. "I want that haughty sister of mine to know that I am marrying a real man."

Jap came swiftly back.

"Have you taken Bill into your confidence, Sis?" he asked, patting Isabel's shoulder gently, as he smiled his whimsical smile at Mabelle.

"You're naughty to tease her so," his wife chided.

"Bill and I are going to New York on our wedding trip, just as soon as Isabel can spare me. I want Fanny Maud to see——" She stopped, then took the bit in her teeth. "Jappie, you never knew why I ran away from New York last Thanksgiving. Of course I told Bill all about it long ago. Fanny and I certainly don't agree when it comes to men. I can't imagine she will approve of Bill, after the one she picked for me."

Further confidence was cut short by the appearance of Bill, turning the corner. She arose and ran to meet him.

"Poor Bill," Jap laughed, as the two came arm in arm up the shady lawn.

Before her designs upon Bill could be executed, a strange thing happened. Fanny Maud and a company of musicians made a summer concert tour. It was only a little run from the city, and such an aggregation of artists as Bloomtown's wildest dreams had never visioned descended upon the town. The hotel was taxed to its uttermost capacity, with six song birds, an orchestra, three lap dogs, and an Impresario whose manner implied that he had designs other than professional on the leading soprano. Her stay was short, and left an impression of perfume, fluffy ruffles, French and haste. Her manager consented to have her sing for Jap and Isabel.

Bloomtown stood out in the road, listening, agape. Perhaps Kelly Jones had been to Barton that summer night, for he declared that cats were climbing out of Tom Granger's chimneys, screeching for help, and a man kept scaring them worse by howling at them. When Fanny Maud reached the famous high note she was justly proud of, Kelly clapped his hands to his stomach and yelled for mercy.

"That's clawsick music," abjured Bill, who was sitting on the lawn with Mabelle. Kelly looked at them with sorrow.

"I was skeered that she had busted her throat, and all the sound was comin' out to onct," he complained.

The last night of the brief but exciting visit Bill and Mabelle were quietly married. Quietly—yes and no. Mike Hawkins rallied the band and all the tinware in town to celebrate. Mabelle was indignant at first, but soon began to enjoy the fun, and created the happiest impression on the older generation of Bloomtown by insisting on marching arm in arm with Kelly Jones at the head of the procession. After Bill had given his solemn oath never to repeat the offense the "chivaree" broke up, with wild yells of congratulation.

They took up residence in Mabelle's cottage. By consensus of opinion it was Mabelle's cottage. The town in fact so thoroughly recognized Mabelle, in the possessive case, that Jap cautioned Bill against the contingency of being referred to as "Mabelle's husband." Bill was proud of his wife, and when fortune brought him lucre, from the long-forgotten bit of Texas land that suddenly showed oil, he began to improve the whole street by putting out trees.

As Jap feelingly declared, Mabelle had even improved the dirt under the doorstep of the cottage, and Bill was fairly pushed out on the street for improving to do. Under her fostering care, Bill had learned to make violent demands on the Town Board. And they, the aldermen of Bloomtown, bent on pursuing the even tenor of their way at any hazard, had to adjust themselves to a new ebullition from Bill every Tuesday night. But Bill and Mabelle were not doomed to see their enthusiasm go up in vapor. It bore, instead, the most substantial fruit. The barren, treeless town was beginning to grow shade for the aldermen to rest under in their old age.

Kelly Jones said that if Jap had brought Mabelle with him, instead of waiting fourteen years to import her, the town would be larger than St. Louis. As it was, Bloomtown might yet run that city a swift race. Mabelle set the fashions; told the School Board how to run the schools; the preachers how to make their churches popular; the mothers how to train their children. And the Town Fathers all carried their hats in their hands when she breezed down the street. Jap and Isabel watched and smiled, serene in the happiness that was theirs.

"How wonderful it is, Jap, dear," said Isabel, standing in the sunset glow, on that Easter Sunday, after the year had flown. The last red gleam touched the tip of the monument to Ellis Hinton, that had been erected by Bloomtown and dedicated that morning. Together they had gone to the cemetery, when the crowd would not be there, Isabel's arms full of garlands for the low green tents of their loved ones.

"It seemed that Flossy must be smiling at you as you stood there, saying the marvelous things that must have come to you direct from the lips of your spirit father. Ellis Hinton spoke through you when you told the story of our town."

Jap drew her tenderly to the fostering shadow of the monument and pressed her to his heart. Her face was glorified as she looked up into his.

"Oh, Jap, what if Ellis had never lived!"

Jap drew her close. Many hours had he wrought with his fear, but now the roses had come again to her cheeks and the light to her eyes. He looked over the City of Peace, and his own eyes were full with joy.

"But, thank God, Ellis did live." And arm in arm they walked back to Ellis Hinton's real town.

As they crossed the railroad tracks, Kelly Jones came ambling down from the station, where a large contingent from the vicinity of the steel highway between Barton and Bloomtown waited for the evening "Accommodation."

"Gimmeny!" he exclaimed, clapping Jap on the shoulder, "I sure was proud of Ellis's boy to-day. Ellis says to me, the day he went away, says he, 'Watch my boy, Kelly. He is goin' to put the electricity in Bloomtown's backbone,' and, by jolly, you done it! I reckon you felt proud," he went on, turning to Isabel, "when Wat Harlow called Jap the man that made Bloomtown a real town, and the crowd yelled, 'Yes.'

Well, ma'am, for a minute I shook and grunted. And then the wife said, 'Wait a bit,' so I waited. And when Jap got up and told the folks that not Jap Herron but a greater man than he ever hoped to be, had cradled and nussed Bloomtown and learnt her to walk, I might' nigh split my guzzle yellin' for joy. Did you hear me yellin', 'Hurrah for Ellis's boy!' And did you hear the crowd say it after me?"

As Isabel took his hardened hand in hers, her eyes overflowed.

"Jap *is* Ellis," she said gently, "to you and to his town. I know it, and I am glad."

CHAPTER XXVI

B<small>ILL</small> sat doubled over the case, the stick held list-lessly in his hand. Nervously he fingered the copy, not knowing what he was reading. From time to time he slid down from the stool and lounged across the big office to the street door. Vacantly he returned the greetings of his townsmen, as he gazed past them, across the corner of the little park that lay, brown and gold, in the glory of Indian Summer, across the intervening street where Tom Granger's sedate old house looked out on the leaf-strewn lawn. He could see Tom Granger, pacing up and down the walk. He could see Jap, sitting under the great elm, his face hidden in his hands.

"Poor old Jap," Bill muttered, brushing aside a tear, as he returned once more to his case, "life has slammed him so many tough licks that he is always cringing, afraid of another lick."

The morning wore on. Bill gave up the effort at type-setting and tried to apply himself to the exchanges, so that he could the better watch the front of that house. He was near the door, trying to read, when, all at once, Tom stopped pacing. Jap sprang up and bounded across the lawn and into the front door. A white-capped nurse ran through the wide hall, and in a little while Mabelle put her head out of an upper window and peered over at the office. Bill pushed his chair back and tramped heavily to the pavement. Then he tramped back again.

"Certainly there are enough of them to let somebody come here with news," he growled. "They don't seem to know that there are telephones—or that I would care."

Half an hour dragged. Then, all alone, his face shining with holy joy, Jap hurried to the office. For a moment neither could speak. Hand in hand, heart beating with heart, they stood looking into each other's eyes. Then Jap said huskily:

"Do you remember what Ellis said, that day when his greatest joy came?"

Bill flung his arms around Jap and hugged him lustily.

" 'Get out all the roosters!' " he cried, tears gushing from his brown eyes.

"And," said Jap slowly, "Isabel wants to call him Jasper William."

THE END

CPSIA information can be obtained
at www.ICGtesting.com
Printed in the USA
JSHW011353170323
39100JS00001B/13